# Ruled Out

# KidWitness Tales

*Crazy Jacob*
by Jim Ware

*Dangerous Dreams*
by Jim Ware

*Galen and Goliath*
by Lee Roddy

*Ruled Out*
by Randy Southern

*Trouble Times Ten*
by Dave Lambert

*The Worst Wish*
by Lissa Halls Johnson

# Ruled Out

### RANDY SOUTHERN

# BETHANYHOUSE
MINNEAPOLIS, MINNESOTA

A Focus on the Family book.
Published by Bethany House Publishers
A Ministry of Bethany Fellowship International
11400 Hampshire Avenue South
Bloomington, Minnesota 55438
www.bethanyhouse.com

Printed in the United States of America by
Bethany Press International, Bloomington, Minnesota 55438

**Library of Congress Cataloging-in-Publication Data**

Southern, Randy.
    Ruled out / Randy Southern.
        p.   cm. — (KidWitness tales)
Summary: Nine-year-old Ethan, one of the Israelites who followed Moses
out of Egypt to Mount Sinai, hates rules and is frustrated when Moses goes
up the mountain to get even more rules from God. But through the
rebellion of others he discovers how rules can be important to keep us safe.
    ISBN 1-56179-884-3
    1. Moses (Biblical leader)—Juvenile fiction. [1. Moses (Biblical
leader)—Fiction. 2. Ten commandments—Fiction. 3. Conduct of life—
Fiction.] I. Title. II. Series.
    PZ7.S72735 Ru 2000
    [Fic]—dc21                                                    00-010712

2  3  4  5  6  7  8  9  10  11  12  13  14  15 / 07  06  05  04  03  02  01

*To Ann, Amy, and Brady*

RANDY SOUTHERN, a former youth product developer for Cook Communications, now works as a freelance writer and editor. His most recent work includes *What Would Jesus Do* (Youth Specialties) and *The Custom Youth Discipleship Series* (Cook).

## CHAPTER 1

CR-RRR-AAA-CK! B-RRRR-UMMMMM!

Lightning exploded overhead, but the blinding flash was quickly swallowed by the thick, dark clouds that covered the top of Mount Sinai. The thunder that followed made its way down the mountain with a low, grumbling sound, shaking rocks loose and sending them tumbling after it.

The ground under Ethan's sandals vibrated with the rumble. *Good one*, he thought. He grinned and held his stomach, which was doing some tumbling of its own. Nobody liked lightning more than Ethan did, and this was *super* lightning.

He glanced around impatiently. Melki was missing all this. *Where is he, anyway? He was supposed to meet me at the boundary marker.*

Ethan started walking up the path again, picking his way through the brambles that had overgrown it. Every so often he lifted his head to stare at the mountain in front of him—a tower that rose suddenly from the flat desert floor, its granite as dark brown and rough and wrinkled-looking as an old man's face. He tried to imagine climbing the sheer cliffs, hand over hand, but the path was the only way up the mountain as far as he could see. Narrowing between two large rocks, it twisted and turned up the side until it disappeared into the clouds that had settled on the peak.

Lightning flashed again, and the thunder clapped a few seconds later. *Close*, Ethan thought, *but not close enough*. He wanted to see the white-hot bolts, the spiky fingers reaching down from the sky. What else was there to do when you were stuck in the middle of a miserable desert, having to follow a bunch of stupid—

"You there!" It was a man's voice, calling from somewhere up the path. Ethan dropped his gaze from the mountaintop and saw a muscular-looking, gray-robed Israelite pop from behind a boulder. "What's your business here?" the man said, scratching his tangle of a beard.

Ethan swallowed. He swallowed again when he saw that the man had a bow in his hand and a quiver of arrows slung on his back.

"I said, what's your business?" the man repeated. "You should be back in camp, boy."

Another man, taller and skinnier than the first, stepped from behind the boulder. He seemed more curious than angry, but Ethan noticed he was armed with bow and arrows, too. "A visitor?" the second man asked.

"Some kid," the first man growled. "The last thing we need."

Ethan glanced back over his shoulder, toward camp. He could see rows and rows of tents, and knots of people here and there, braving the desert sun. But he didn't see Melki.

He groaned. Melki was good at stuff like this, standing up to adults and speaking his mind. It usually got Melki into trouble, but maybe getting in trouble was better than being a meek little sheep. Lately Ethan was getting tired of being a sheep.

He cleared his throat, which felt as rough and dry as the mountain in front of him looked. "Is—is the boundary around here?" he asked.

The first man raised his bow and pointed it further up the path. Ethan could see a pile of a dozen or so large stones stacked on top of each other. "That's the marker," the man said gruffly.

Ethan wrinkled his nose. *Not exactly what I expected.* The adults had made such a big deal of the boundary, he'd almost thought the marker would look like one of the giant stone archways they'd left back in Egypt, guarded by statues of weird-looking animals or dead pharaohs. But it was just a pile of rocks.

"You've gone as far as you need to go, boy," the first man warned.

The taller man looked at Ethan, giving him an aren't-you-a-cute-child smile that made Ethan wince. "In case you haven't heard, son, God has told Moses that no one is to go up the mountain."

*I heard*, Ethan thought. *Everybody who hasn't been in a cave for the last week has heard.*

"So you're . . . guarding the boundary?" Ethan ventured.

"That's the general idea," said the first man, reaching back over his shoulder and pulling an arrow from the quiver. He fitted the arrow to the bowstring and narrowed his eyes at Ethan.

Ethan gulped.

The taller man frowned at his companion. "Come on," he scolded. "You're gonna scare him. He's just a boy." He turned toward Ethan. "How old are you, son? Eight?"

Ethan felt his cheeks turn red. "Nine and a half," he mumbled.

"Well, I'm sure your family has chores for you to do. Run along, now. Got to follow the rules, you know."

Ethan clenched his teeth at the word. Rules.

*That's all we have anymore.* Kicking a stone off the path, he turned and slowly started walking back toward camp.

He hadn't gone far when another lightning flash lit up the sky. He turned to the mountain, but couldn't see anything through the clouds. Disappointed, he stood there as the thunder echoed in his ears.

"Hey," came a sudden voice from behind him. "Guess I'm a little late, huh?"

Whirling, Ethan saw Melki standing in the middle of the path. "A *little* late?" Ethan cried. "I had to stand up to the boundary guards myself. They have bows and arrows and—"

Melki snorted. "Oooh, I'm scared. What are they, a couple of guys who used to make bricks in Egypt? Not exactly soldiers. They probably couldn't hit the broad side of a pyramid with their arrows."

Ethan looked up at the sky, searching in vain for more lightning. "Maybe not. But they won't let us get any closer. We'll have to watch from here."

Melki sighed long and loud, but found a broad, flat rock where they could sit. They waited in silence for a minute or so, until lightning flared again behind the clouds.

After the thunder faded, Ethan glanced over at his best friend, who was poking a stick into a crack in the rock. "Could you see it *that* time?"

"Just barely," Melki answered, obviously unimpressed. "I'm telling you, we need to get closer if we *really* want to see."

"We can't *get* any closer!" Ethan said. "The boundary marker's right up there. It's just a pile of rocks, but—"

Melki shook his head. "A pile of rocks!" He picked up a handful of sand and threw it toward the mountain. "All we have to do is walk *around* it." He pointed to a small plateau several hundred feet up the mountainside. "That's where we need to go. We could lie on our backs and stare up through the bottom of the clouds. We'd be able to see *everything!*"

Ethan looked over at his friend. *Wish I could be more like Melki,* he thought. It wasn't just that Melki seemed older, even though they were the same age and almost the same height. It wasn't just that Melki's dark hair was curly and wild, as if someone had just spilled it on top of his head, and Ethan's was straight and neatly groomed and boring. It wasn't just that Melki was broad and muscular, like his father, and Ethan was thin and wiry, like *his* father.

It was the fact that Melki didn't have to worry about . . . rules.

"You know we're not supposed to go past the marker," Ethan said, then made a sour face. He didn't like the words that were coming out of his mouth. And he *especially* didn't like saying them to Melki. "We have to stay off the mountain until the Lord talks to Moses. You know the rules."

"Rules!" Melki roared with laughter. "Do you know who you're starting to sound like?" He lifted his head as high as he could, puffed his chest out, and started stroking an imaginary beard. "Ethan, you know the rules," he said in a deep, stern voice. "You can't eat manna that other families have collected. You can't leave our tent area on the Sabbath. And you can't go to the bathroom after sundown."

Ethan snickered, then lowered his head to hide his smile. Melki's imitation of Father was perfect, but it didn't seem right to encourage him. "You know my father doesn't have a rule about going to the bathroom."

"Maybe not yet," Melki answered. "But give him time. He has rules for everything else—you said so yourself."

Ethan sighed. "Yeah, but the rule about the mountain didn't come from my father. It came from Moses." He glanced up to see the end of a lightning flash, then looked down again. "He said we can't set foot on it because God is there, and God is holy. Besides, even if we wanted to climb the mountain, we couldn't. *They* wouldn't let us." He pointed back over his shoulder toward the guards. "That path is the only way up this side of the mountain, and there's no way we could get past them without getting caught."

"We could if we did it at night," Melki whispered. "There's a lot more to see here at night anyway."

"How do you know?" Ethan demanded.

"I snuck out of our tent last night and came over here," Melki answered. He gave Ethan a sly smile.

Ethan looked up and down the path to make sure no one was coming or going. "Are you crazy?" he hissed, keeping his voice low even though no one else was in sight. "Did you—"

"*No*, I didn't go on the mountain," Melki finished. "But I could have. There was only one guard by the boundary marker, and I think he was asleep. But I knew you would want to go with me, so I decided to wait until you were there."

*Well, that's kind of nice*, Ethan thought, sitting a little taller. *Melki never waits for anything. Kind of like Leah—*

*Leah!* he thought, suddenly remembering. "Uh-oh," he said. "My sister's probably waiting for me." He got up from the rock. "I'm supposed to meet her by the dead tree, near the stream."

Melki rolled his eyes, but got up, too. "Let's go," he said. "Wouldn't want to keep Leah the Law Lover waiting."

Sweat was trickling down Ethan's neck and into the scratchy collar of his robe by the time they reached the northern border of the camp. It was nearing the hottest part of the day, and the clouds around Mount Sinai didn't reach far enough to block the sun. At least being skinny made it easy for Ethan to wind his way through the tight maze of tents, cooking fires, and people. Melki followed, mumbling about the heat and how it had never seemed this hot back in Egypt.

Ethan looked around at the tents, row after row of goatskin shelters in various shades of tan and gray. None of them flapped even a little in the breezeless air. He was glad the Israelites had been in the Sinai Valley for only a few days—not long enough for the camp to take on the sharp, stomach-turning odor of sweat, boiling manna, and animal waste mingled together. But he knew that smell would come soon enough. It always did.

The sun was directly overhead now. Ethan could feel it baking his scalp. "Leah's going to be mad," he said. "She told me not to be late, because she didn't have time to wait for me today."

Melki snorted again. "Oh, then we'd better *hurry*," he said, and proceeded to plop himself down right in the middle of the path to the dead tree.

Ethan's heart seemed to squeeze in his chest. "What are you *doing?*" he asked, looking around to make sure no one was coming. "Get up!"

"No," Melki said. "Leah may be *your* master, but she's not mine."

"What are you talking about?" Ethan cried. He could feel his face turning red. "Leah's not my master."

Melki rolled his eyes and shook his head. "*Everybody's* your master," he said with a laugh. "Your father, your mother, your sister, and everyone else who tells you what to do. They say, 'Do this,' and you do it. They say, 'Don't do this,' and you don't do it. It's like you're still a slave."

"I'm as free as you are," Ethan said. He wanted it to sound like a challenge, but it came out sounding more like a question.

Melki stood up and took a step toward him. "Have you ever told your father how much you hate it out here in the desert, or that you wish you'd never left Egypt?" he asked.

"No," Ethan answered, looking down at the sand. "Have you?"

Melki laughed. "My father and I talk about it all the time. He hates the wilderness as much as I do! My mother does, too."

"Yeah, but I can't talk to *my* family about things like that," Ethan muttered.

"Why not?" Melki asked. "Because you're afraid

of getting beaten or yelled at, like when you were a slave in Egypt?"

"No," Ethan answered. He knew his parents would never beat him, and they rarely raised their voices. But that didn't mean he was free to break the rules, did it?

"A free person can do whatever he wants—including climbing that mountain," Melki explained. "A slave does what he's told and follows other people's rules. So does that make you a free person or a slave?"

Ethan saw a quick vision of himself being led around by three chains—one held by his father, one by his mother, and one by his sister. He closed his eyes and shook his head, trying to erase the image from his mind. "Just drop it, okay?" he told Melki.

Melki laughed again and grabbed Ethan's arm. "Come on, slave. Your master—I mean, your sister— is waiting."

Ethan dug his sandal into the path, then kicked sand in Melki's direction. *He's right*, Ethan thought. *I'm not just mad because he said I'm a slave. I'm mad because he's right.*

Long before they reached the dead tree, Ethan could see Leah waiting. There was her profile—the nose that stuck out a little too far, the chin that didn't stick out far enough. She was squinting the way she usually did. Altogether she reminded Ethan of some homely, nearsighted bird.

No wonder nobody likes her, he thought. *And she just makes it worse with the way she acts.*

The closer they got, the more clearly Ethan could see his frowning sister scouring the horizon for a sign of him. Finally her squint settled on the two boys, and her frown deepened. She shook her head as they approached.

*Don't give me a lecture in front of Melki*, Ethan warned silently. *And don't tell me how disappointed you are. You're not my mother.*

Sometimes it was hard to remember that himself. Even though Leah was only two years older than he was, Ethan often felt as if he had three parents—the shortest of whom constantly lectured him about rules. The fact that Leah looked a lot like their mother, with her almond-shaped eyes and wavy, black hair, didn't help.

"You promised you would be here *before* midday," Leah said, her voice nasal and piercing. "Remember Father's rule. When you make a promise to someone, you must always keep it."

Ethan bit his tongue and tried not to look at Melki. He could feel himself blushing again.

Leah picked up a bundle of bone-white clothes from the ground and threw it at Ethan. He lurched to catch it, but it fell to the sand.

"What's that?" Melki asked.

Leah looked at Melki as if a locust were crawling out of his nose. "It's Ethan's Sabbath outfit," she explained. "We're on our way to the stream to make our clothes clean—like Moses told us to do."

Melki snickered. "My father said we didn't have to clean *our* clothes again, since we just washed them a week ago."

Leah ignored him and turned to Ethan. "We have to go *now*. Mother and Father are already at the stream waiting for us." She shook her head at Melki and started off toward the stream.

Melki just grinned at her. "Leah the Law Lover," he said. "She's got you trained, that's for sure."

Ethan set his jaw and bent down to pick up the clothes. "I'll see you later," he said. "Come by our tent after supper tonight." He started to follow Leah, but Melki grabbed his arm.

"Don't be a slave your whole life," Melki whispered. "Do something *you* want to do." Then he pointed to the mountain and smiled.

Just then the lightning flashed. "I'll think about it," Ethan replied as he started off after Leah. "You can count on that."

## CHAPTER 2

When he caught up with Leah, Ethan fell into step beside her—but said nothing. Suddenly she turned to him with a big smile on her face, and he got a sinking feeling in the pit of his stomach. Anything that could make her smile like that was bound to be bad news for him.

"I almost forgot to tell you what Father said," she announced. She said it so loudly and so excitedly that an old man who was nursing a lamb's injured leg nearby looked up from his work.

"What?" Ethan asked, grabbing her arm to keep her moving.

"He said the Lord is going to give Moses a whole new set of rules for us to follow!" She grinned at him expectantly, as if she thought he might do a little celebration dance.

Ethan stopped dead in his tracks, startling an old woman who was boiling manna near the path. "*More* rules?" He spat out each word as though it were a bad taste in his mouth. "We don't *need* more rules. We have too many rules *now!*"

"You won't think that way after you learn to follow them," Leah said, looking down her nose at him.

"Don't you ever feel like you're a slave to rules?" For a moment Ethan wasn't sure whether he'd asked the question out loud or just thought it. Then he saw Leah's eyebrows bunch together in confusion.

"What are you *talking* about?" she asked.

His grip tightened on the bundle of clothes in his hands. "Don't you ever get tired of doing what you're told?" he asked. "Don't you ever feel like thinking for yourself?"

She frowned. "Are you saying you're wiser than Moses? Wiser than God? That you can come up with better rules on your own?"

He stared at the mountain in the distance. "I could come up with *fewer* rules, that's for sure."

Leah folded her arms across her chest. "I suppose you liked it better in Egypt. Some people do, I hear. Maybe you liked the Egyptians' rules better, and their false gods."

*You just don't get it, do you?* he thought. He waved his arm around at the rows and rows of tents. "Don't you ever wish you were back there? I mean, look! This is the desert! We live in tents! Don't you remember what it was like in Egypt? We had actual *furniture!* Real food, not just manna that we have to scrape off the ground every day! Sure, it tastes kind of like honey, but anybody would get sick of honey after a while—"

"Don't *you* remember what it was like in Egypt?" she shot back. "We were *slaves* there!"

"And we're *still* slaves," Ethan said. "Slaves to rules. And where have the rules gotten us? To the middle of nowhere, with nothing to do but . . . sweat and argue."

"Well, you should know," Leah said, making a face. "Those are the two things you do best." She turned and headed down the path toward the stream.

Shaking his head, Ethan followed. "Just forget it," he mumbled, disgusted. "You wouldn't understand anyway."

The stream was barely a trickle, at least compared with what Ethan remembered of the Nile River in Egypt. This water was no more than eight feet wide at any point, and barely rose above the ankles of the people who stood in it, washing their clothes.

Ethan saw his mother standing in the middle of the stream, smiling and waving her arms over her head to get his attention. He took off his sandals and left them on the bank. He could hear Leah splashing along behind him as he made his way into the rippling, sun-warmed water.

His bare feet sank in the wet sand as he passed at least a half dozen families who were washing their clothes together. It seemed strange to see men, women, and children washing side by side. Usually only the women cleaned clothes.

Ethan's mother cupped a handful of water and gave him a playful splash when he got close. Behind her, his father grunted and strained as he rubbed his grayish cloak on a rock in the stream. Sweat poured from his dark hair down the side of his long, thin face. He seemed to be concentrating hard and didn't look up.

*It's a good thing he doesn't wash clothes very often*, Ethan thought. *He'd rub holes in everything.*

Ethan walked over and knelt in the water next to his father. After scrubbing his robe against the rock for a few seconds, Ethan broke the silence. "Uh . . . there sure is a lot of lightning on the mountain today," he said.

His father kept rubbing his own cloak against the rock, seeming not to hear.

Ethan tried again. "Father, how dangerous is the mountain?"

Finally his father looked up and seemed to notice Ethan for the first time. "Hmm? The mountain?" He turned toward Mount Sinai. "It's only dangerous to those who don't follow the Lord's commands."

It was the kind of thing Ethan had heard him say many times. Ethan wasn't surprised when Leah came splashing over to listen, either.

"Think of it as a scorpion," his father continued. "If you treat it with respect and keep your distance, it isn't dangerous."

Ethan nodded and slapped his robe against the rock. The coarse material felt even rougher when it was wet, and the folded edges scratched his hands and forearms.

His father watched for a few moments, then spoke. "Ethan, you need to put more effort into your work. Your clothes should be cleaner than they were the day you first wore them."

"Tell him *why*, Father," Leah urged. For a moment Ethan wanted to slap *her* against the rock.

"The Lord Himself has come to meet with Moses," his father explained. "He wants us to be ready for Him. The way we make ourselves look on the *outside* will show how much we care on the *inside*."

Ethan stopped washing and stood up straight. "Melki's father said *his* family didn't have to wash their clothes again since they washed them last week."

His father drew himself up, too—in a way that always made him look about a foot taller than he actually was. He began stroking his beard. Ethan thought of Melki's impression and tried not to smile.

"Did Melki's father change Pharaoh's heart and convince him to let our people leave Egypt?" Father asked.

"No," Ethan answered.

"Did Melki's father lead us in battle against the Amalekites?"

"No."

"Did Melki's father hold back the waters of the Red Sea so that we could cross over on dry ground?"

"No."

His father took a step toward Ethan and leaned in close—so close that their noses were almost touching. "That's why *my* family is going to listen to the *Lord*, and not to *Melki's father*," he said.

His voice was so intense it seemed to bore a hole between Ethan's eyes. Without another word, Father went back to his cloak-washing.

In the distance, thunder rumbled from the top of Mount Sinai. Ethan turned toward the cloud-covered peak and stared. The longer he looked at the mountain, the more he wanted to be there.

He replayed Melki's words in his head: *Do something* you *want to do.*

"Do you want to be a slave your entire life?" his best friend had asked.

*No,* Ethan told himself. *One way or another, I'm going to be free.*

## CHAPTER 3

Next morning, after breakfast, Ethan stood by his family's tent. He could still taste the manna in his mouth. *Yuck*, he thought. *Will I be eating this every day for the rest of my life?* He longed for the bread they'd had back in Egypt—puffy, golden loaves made with oil and poked full of holes, sending out a rich, fresh smell when his mother slid them from the brick oven. Even flatbread would taste good now, thin and chewy with a piece of roast lamb tucked inside . . .

Shaking his head and trying to forget, Ethan gazed at the mountain. There was something different about the lightning today. The flashes seemed to come more often. He could imagine himself with Melki, looking up through those clouds. *We could see everything up close,* he thought.

He turned to his father, who was shaking sand from one of the sleeping mats. "Do you think we'll be allowed on the mountain after today?" Ethan asked. He tried to keep his voice casual, as though the question had just popped into his head. Picking up a rock, he tossed it on the sloped part of the tent roof and caught it when it rolled down.

His father tossed the mat inside the tent, then straightened up. "Why are you so curious about the mountain?" he asked. "Three times now I've told you that Mount Sinai is forbidden ground, yet you still ask me about it. What do you have in mind, son?"

Ethan froze. What could he say? He hated to lie to his father. But if he told him the truth about what he and Melki were planning, there would be a different kind of lightning storm to worry about.

"I was just—" Ethan started, but suddenly his words were drowned out by a sound unlike any that had ever met his ears.

It was a blare, a blast that seemed to come from the top of Mount Sinai. At first he thought it was thunder, but the noise was too shrill and high-pitched, a sort of squeal but more powerful. It echoed crazily throughout the valley, making it seem as though it were coming from 10 directions at once.

"That's it!" his father said excitedly. "Moses said a trumpet blast would be our signal." He reached toward the rest of the family. "It's time to go to the mountain! Stay together!"

*A trumpet?* Ethan wondered. *What kind of trumpet makes a sound like that?* It didn't sound like any ram's horn he'd ever heard.

But it didn't matter. What counted was that he was going to the mountain. Maybe he could get closer this time. Maybe when it was over, he could go further up the path, even to the plateau with Melki.

The walk to the mountain was too long, too slow. No one else seemed to be in a hurry. Most of the people acted nervous, even scared, as they made their way toward Sinai. Ethan had to match their trudging pace.

Worst of all, he wasn't anywhere near the front of the crowd. *I'll never get to hear Moses*, he thought. It was always like this when he was at the back of the crowd on the way to an important camp meeting. With about two million people in front of him, he could never tell what was going on.

Just as he'd feared, the journey ended about a quarter mile from the base of the mountain, near a small foothill. This was as close as they were going to get to Mount Sinai.

Ethan scrambled to the top of the foothill and looked around. Even though the hill was no more than eight feet high, he could see quite a distance across the Sinai Valley.

*Not bad*, he thought. *I wonder if Melki can see me up here.* He waved at the crowd around him, just in case Melki was watching. *I hope so. He'd be so jealous.*

People were pouring into the valley from all directions. The way they moved reminded Ethan of the waves on the Red Sea. "The Israelite Sea," he said to himself.

"The Israelites see *what?*" came a voice right behind him. It was Leah.

"What are *you* doing up here?" Ethan cried. "This is *my* spot!"

"Father told us to stay together," she explained. "That's the rule, so that's what I'm doing!"

Ethan gritted his teeth when he heard the word *rule*. For a moment he could see himself giving Leah a shove and watching her roll down the hill. Sure, there would be a couple million witnesses—but if they knew what Leah was like, he thought, they would probably cheer him on.

Just then he noticed that his sister was staring at something in the sky behind him. When he turned back toward the mountain, it took his brain a few seconds to register what he was seeing.

The clouds on top of Mount Sinai appeared to be . . . *melting.*

Dark wisps drifted slowly down the mountainside like a creeping fog. Even in the heat a chill ran down

Ethan's spine, and he felt the hair on the back of his neck begin to rise.

Soon he saw that the dark fog wasn't a cloud at all—it was smoke. Within a minute it had blanketed the entire mountain in blackness.

The trumpet blasted again, this time so loudly his ears hurt. From his perch on the hill Ethan noticed a ripple of movement at the front of the crowd. He guessed that people were trying to back away from the mountain. *Cowards*, he thought, then noticed that his own palms were getting sweaty.

In the midst of the smoke, just barely visible through the dark billows, he saw an orange glow and flickering yellow lights. It was as if the dead rock of the mountain had caught fire.

*How can that be?* Ethan wondered. *And what does all this have to do with God coming down?*

His head started to swim. The weird sights and sounds were starting to come a little too fast. He could hear Leah gasping behind him.

Trying to calm down, he looked away from the mountain—and spotted movement out of the corner of his eye. About 100 paces to the east, a lone figure stepped out of the crowd and walked toward the smoky mountain. Ethan's breath caught in his throat as he recognized the long, silver beard and the white cloak with up-and-down purple stripes.

"It's Moses!" he called down to his parents.

"Moses?" a woman in the crowd asked. "What's he doing?"

"He's walking toward the mountain," Ethan called out. "Now he's standing still, looking up."

The people around the foothill murmured expectantly. Ethan stood taller, proud to be the bearer of such important news. He'd never gotten closer than 50 feet to Moses, but this was almost as good as seeing him face to face.

Just then a new sound roared from the mountain, louder than the trumpet. It seemed to come from the fire at the middle of Mount Sinai. It started as a *whoosh* of wind, like the one Ethan remembered hearing when the waters of the Red Sea parted. Then came quick bursts of thunder like the pounding of giant drums. Each burst rattled the mountainside and shook the ground under Ethan's feet. His knees started to buckle.

"The voice of God!" someone cried out. "The Lord is speaking to Moses!"

Ethan's heart thumped wildly in his chest. Was it really God's voice? For months his father had been telling him that the Lord was leading the Israelites across the wilderness. But Ethan had never seen the Lord nor heard Him speak.

The booming sound echoed throughout the valley.

Ethan squeezed his eyes shut, straining to make out anything that might sound like words. But before he could, the sound stopped—just as abruptly as it had started.

Opening his eyes, Ethan watched as the black smoke that encircled Mount Sinai rose like a curtain. Soon it vanished into the dark clouds on top of the mountain.

A lightning flash lit up the whole valley. Ethan could see that Moses was now facing the crowd, gesturing broadly.

Feeling dizzy, Ethan took a deep breath. "I think Moses is saying something," he called down to the crowd below. But he was too far away to hear what Moses was saying. They would all have to wait for the message to be relayed back to them.

Whatever Moses said, it didn't take very long. After a couple of minutes, he turned back toward the mountain and knelt. Ethan couldn't tell for sure, but it looked like Moses was adjusting his sandals.

Leah grabbed Ethan's arm. "Look," she said, "the people closest to the mountain are starting to pass Moses' message back." Ethan watched as the message made its way through the crowd. As soon as one section of people heard it, a dozen or so of them would spread out to share it with other parts of the crowd.

Finally, after what seemed like hours, a short,

chubby teenage boy in a green robe elbowed his way through the crowd to the foothill where Ethan and Leah were standing. Huffing and puffing his way to the top, the young man held out his hands for silence.

"This is what the Lord says," he began in a high, raspy voice. 'Be careful that you do not go up the mountain or touch the foot of it. Whoever touches the mountain shall surely be put to death. He shall surely be stoned or shot with arrows; not a hand is to be laid on him. Whether man or animal, he shall not be permitted to live.' "

Ethan frowned, remembering the guards at the boundary. *Stoned or shot with arrows—just for setting foot on the mountain!* he protested silently. *It's not fair!*

Wondering how Melki was taking the news, he turned and noticed Leah whispering to herself: "Not a hand is to be laid on him . . . whether man or animal . . . not permitted to live."

He groaned. She was memorizing the new rule— the same way she memorized *every* new rule that God or Moses or Father or anyone else came up with. Before long she'd be reciting this new rule to him every time he walked within 300 paces of Mount Sinai.

The teenage messenger finished his speech with one last piece of news: "The Lord has called his servant Moses to the top of the mountain."

Ethan heard someone at the bottom of the foothill gasp, and wondered why. *I'd* love *to climb the mountain!* he thought. *Just think of all the great stuff Moses will get to see.*

The young messenger brushed past Ethan and Leah, then hurried down the hill to spread the news to another part of camp.

Ethan turned back toward the mountain, just in time to see Moses head slowly up the path. Ethan remembered Melki's words about the boundary marker: "All we have to do is walk *around* it."

*Only if your name is Moses*, Ethan thought, digging the front end of his sandal in the dirt.

A crash of thunder echoed across the valley. When the echo faded, Ethan heard the people around him talking. They sounded scared.

"Moses is an old man," a woman said. "What if something happens to him on the mountain?"

"What if he gets struck by lightning?" a man asked. "Who would lead us then?"

"Where would we go?" another man joined in. "Back to Egypt? We would all be killed."

Ethan looked around for his father, expecting him to say something comforting like, "The Lord will protect us." But his father was gone.

Leah must have noticed him looking around. "Father went to tell the people behind us about the Lord's new rule," she said, putting extra emphasis on the last two words.

Ethan looked back at the jagged cliffs and steep slopes of Mount Sinai. *Maybe those grown-ups are right*, he thought. *I'll bet there are a lot of places where an old man could fall and hurt himself.* He glanced around at the adults' worried faces. *What if something happens to Moses up there? If no one else is allowed on the mountain, he'd just lie there until he died.*

The more Ethan thought about it, the more his stomach knotted. *What if Moses does die? How will anyone know it? How long will we wait for him to come down? Until we all die of hunger or thirst?*

He pictured himself lying at the base of Mount Sinai, too weak from hunger to move, his tongue swollen and dry in his mouth, while scorpions crawled over his sun-blistered body.

*Why did God have to send us out here?* he wondered. *And why did He take away the only person who can get us out of the desert alive?*

Then another thought struck him. Maybe it's all because of those stupid rules, wasn't it? Maybe God is like Leah. Maybe He cares more about rules than He does about people.

"I hope you make it back, Moses," Ethan said under his breath. "You're all we've got, and I'm too young to die."

"ome on, Ethan, use your strength," his father encouraged. "Pull harder!"

Ethan grunted, wishing there were something more fun to do than adjust the tent after last night's sandstorm. Two weeks had passed since Moses' climb up the mountain, and the whole camp seemed to be marking time with busy work, anxiously waiting to see whether the Israelite leader would return.

Ethan gritted his teeth, dug his heels into the sandy ground, and tugged at the goatskin strap as hard as he could. The tent flap barely budged. A trickle of sweat rolled down his forehead and into his eye.

The tent peg was right there. If he could just . . . stretch . . . the flap . . . a little . . . further . . .

The muscles in his arms quivered, begging him to stop. He relaxed just for a second, then yanked backward with a loud "Aaauuuggghhh!"

The back of his hand brushed past the wooden

ground peg. He fumbled to get the strap around it. Once, twice, three times he wrapped the strap around the peg—then tied it off with a double knot, just as his father had shown him.

"How's that?" he panted, looking up.

His father knelt next to the tent peg and gave the strap a couple of hard tugs. "No sandstorm is going to blow this knot apart," he said with a smile.

A warm feeling grew in Ethan's chest. "Now all we need to do is clear out the sand that blew in last night," Ethan said. He expected a surprised look from his father and got it. Ethan volunteered to do extra work about as often as he asked for second helpings of manna—which was almost never. But today was different. Today his father had given him a man's job to do—busy work or not—and Ethan had done it. He tried to stop himself from grinning, but couldn't.

His father looked at him, then started to grin, too. "If you're that anxious to work, you can help me find a piece of wood to use for a new tent peg, something that we can carve into a point." He paused and looked at the tent. "But let's get some water first. I think you've earned it."

Ethan jumped to get the pitcher, but his father stopped him. "Stay there—I'll get it." It was Ethan's turn to be surprised. His father fetched water about as often as Ethan volunteered for extra work.

"You have a lot of strength, Ethan," his father called from inside the tent. Ethan looked down at his arms. He'd always thought they were scrawny, but the more he looked at them now, the more muscular they seemed.

His father returned with a clay pitcher and a cup made from a hollowed-out piece of driftwood, a souvenir from the Red Sea. He poured water into the cup and handed it to Ethan. Ethan wanted to gulp it down as quickly as he could, but instead he sipped it slowly, the way his father did.

"Your strength isn't all in your arms, though," his father continued. "It's here." He touched Ethan's forehead. "And here." He pointed to Ethan's heart. "Moses has been on the mountain for two weeks now, and people are starting to get restless. Some might try to tell you what to think or do. Don't let them. Use the strength inside you to resist them."

Ethan nodded his head—not because he understood exactly what his father was saying, but because he knew it was the response his father wanted.

"The only guidance you need is the Lord's commands," his father finished.

Ethan stiffened. He knew "the Lord's commands" was a fancy way of referring to the rules that made him feel like a slave. But this time he resisted the urge to roll his eyes and sigh. If his father was going to treat him like a young man, the least Ethan could do was act like one.

"I need to tell you something." The words were out of Ethan's mouth before he knew they coming.

"What's that?" his father asked.

*I'm tired of doing what other people tell me to do, so Melki and I are going to climb up Mount Sinai, even though Moses said not to. I'm going to sneak out of our tent some night and meet Melki at the boundary marker. Then the two of us are going to follow the path up the mountain until we get high enough to see the lightning.*

Those were the words that were coming. Ethan could feel them.

*Melki's going to kill me*, he thought.

"Melki and I—" Ethan started.

"Father! Father!" Leah came running around the side of the tent. Her face was red and she had little beads of perspiration on her upper lip. She struggled to spit out her message between gasps of breath. "Elizah the Judge . . . sent me to find you. . . . He said there's going to be . . . trouble at the boundary marker. . . . He wants you . . . to meet him there."

Ethan jumped to his feet. Trouble at the boundary marker? It had to be Melki. *I'll bet he tried to climb the mountain without me and got caught*, Ethan thought.

His father handed the clay pitcher to Leah, then hurried off toward Mount Sinai without a word. Leah gave Ethan an excited smile and said, "I feel so honored. Elizah said he was giving *me* the message because he knew I could be trusted to deliver it."

Ethan snorted, but didn't bother coming up with a reply. All he could think of was Melki being held prisoner by a mob of angry Israelites.

He shoved his water cup into Leah's hand. "Hold this," he said. "I've got to get to the boundary marker."

He jogged after his father—not fast enough to catch up with him, but fast enough to keep him in sight. He was afraid that if his father saw him, he'd send him home. And Ethan *had* to know what was happening at the foot of Mount Sinai.

"Don't get in trouble!" Leah called out behind him.

*Don't tell me what to do*, Ethan thought. *You're not my master.*

Keeping one eye on his father and one on the mountain, he made his way through camp. As he'd done for two weeks, he studied each cliff and rock for a sign of Moses. As always, he saw nothing. Dark gray clouds still covered the peak; thunder still rumbled, growing louder as he got closer.

The scene at the foot of Mount Sinai was not

what he'd expected. There was no angry mob holding Melki, or anyone else, prisoner—just a group of about 40 men talking in low voices. Some looked excited, as though they couldn't wait for whatever was about to happen. Others looked angry.

Ethan saw his father talking to a couple of men who had scowls on their faces. One was a small, white-haired man who kept pointing to the mountain with one hand and shaking his fist with the other. *Must be Elizah the Judge*, Ethan decided. His father was nodding in agreement with whatever the old man was saying.

Ethan crept forward as far as he dared, being careful to stay behind large rocks as he moved. Just as he got close enough to hear what the men were saying, they all stopped talking.

His eyes widened. *They spotted me!* he thought. Flattening his body against a rock, he tried to will himself to become invisible.

"Men of Israel," a voice boomed out, "I stand before you today with unpleasant news."

Ethan peeked around the rock and breathed a sigh of relief when he saw that no one was looking at him. Instead, all had turned their attention to the speaker, a tall man in a fancy blue robe who was standing next to the boundary marker.

Ethan noticed the man's clean-shaven face. *Uh-oh,*

*he's an Egyptianite*, Ethan thought. *Father's definitely not going to like him.* "Egyptianite" was the name Ethan's father used to describe Israelites who he thought tried to look and act like Egyptians.

"It's time to choose a new leader!" the man continued. "Moses has been on the mountain for over two weeks now—and for what? More rules? We have more than enough rules already! What we need is food and drink—and the land that was promised to us!"

Ethan gasped, then held his breath. *He's reading my mind!* he thought.

"Moses speaks for the Lord," called a voice from the crowd. "*He* is our leader." Ethan couldn't tell who had spoken, but from the way people turned toward the white-haired man, he assumed it had been Elizah.

The blue-robed man next to the boundary seemed to expect that response. "How do we *know* Moses speaks for the Lord?" he asked. "We all heard the same sound when the cloud came down the mountain, but only Moses understood it. Or, should I say, only Moses *pretended* to understand it."

*Pretended to understand?*

Ethan blinked, trying to make sense of the words. Was that what had happened? Was Moses . . . a fake?

But if Moses was only *pretending* to understand what the Lord was saying, how could he know for sure where to lead the Israelites? Ethan looked down at the dry desert sand. *Maybe this isn't where we're supposed to be.* That thought made his stomach seem to fall, fast. All of a sudden he felt very lost.

*Hey, wait a minute!* he thought. *If Moses wasn't really speaking for the Lord, then the laws he gave us weren't really from God. If they weren't from God, there's no reason to follow them. That would mean, I've been a slave to rules for nothing! I'm free to do whatever I want!*

Lightning lit up the sky overhead. *What if he's right?* Ethan thought as he watched the man talk.

"The laws Moses has given us make no sense," the man was telling the crowd. "He has us scared of this mountain for no reason. *Nothing* is going to happen if we cross this boundary line."

The man took a step toward the mountain. Ethan watched, open-mouthed. From where he stood, the man appeared to be no more than a few inches away from the boundary line.

"Do not cross that boundary, Jeru!" This time Ethan saw that it *was* Elizah who spoke. "The Lord has given us His commands, and we will obey. If you cross that line, *you will be stoned to death.*" The tone of the judge's voice made it clear that he was not bluffing.

Jeru's eyebrows rose. He turned slowly back to

the crowd and glanced at a group of men on his left. They gave him some kind of hand signal that Ethan couldn't see very well. Jeru nodded, then turned to where Elizah and Ethan's father were standing.

"You are a respected elder, Elizah," Jeru said with a smile that made Ethan think he didn't really mean it. "So I will honor your request today. But since you are one of the leaders of our people, I will ask you to consider what I have said."

Elizah said nothing. Ethan couldn't see the old man's face, but he could picture the judge staring angrily at Jeru. The Egyptianite stared back for a moment or two, then threw up his hands and walked away with six or seven men from the crowd. The rest of the group watched in silence before starting home themselves.

Ethan leaned back against the stone, his mind racing. *What if Jeru is right? Are we following rules we don't have to? Would the men really have stoned Jeru to death just for crossing the boundary line?*

Ethan heard footsteps approaching and hunkered down. "This is just the first battle, Amon," Elizah said on the other side of the rock. Ethan peered out just in time to see his father and the judge walk past. "I'm afraid things are only going to get worse around here until Moses returns."

If *he returns*, Ethan thought.

He watched as his father walked toward the camp. The back of his tunic was soaked with sweat, probably from running to meet Elizah.

In his hand, his father held a large, round rock.

When Ethan realized what the rock had been meant for, he shivered.

How big of a piece are we looking for?" Melki asked. He picked up a chunk of tree bark and threw it at Ethan.

Ethan caught the bark with one hand and chucked it back at Melki. "I don't know—big enough to carve a tent peg from." He brushed sand away from the end of a buried branch.

"Well, if we can't find it here, I don't think we'll find it anywhere," Melki said. "This is probably the only dead tree within a hundred miles."

Ethan looked around. Melki was right. There was plenty of mountain and sand to go around, but wood was pretty scarce in the desert. "I think I found something here," he said as he tried to wedge his fingers under the buried branch. "Give me a hand."

"What happens if we don't find the right piece of wood? Is your father going to *stone* us to death?"

Ethan looked up so quickly, he almost lost his

balance. Melki was staring at him with a sarcastic gleam in his eye.

"How do you know about that?" Ethan asked. "It just happened yesterday."

"Word travels fast in this camp," Melki answered.

"How did you find out?" Ethan demanded.

"Calm down, son," Melki said as he knelt next to Ethan and started digging out the other side of the branch. "If you must know, Jeru told my father about it."

"Your father knows *Jeru?*" After Ethan asked the question, he realized how harsh it sounded.

Melki lifted his chin defiantly. "Yeah, he knows Jeru! They grew up together in Egypt. Is that any worse than your father knowing people like Elizah, who would stone someone to death just for saying what's on his mind?"

"Jeru was getting ready to cross the boundary line," Ethan said. "I was there—I saw it."

"Aren't *we* getting ready to cross the boundary line?" Melki asked. "Do you think *we* deserve to die if we go through with our plan?"

Ethan looked down, watching his fingers dig in the sand. He wasn't sure what to say. The mountain was as inviting as ever, and not just because of the lightning. Each day it seemed more like a symbol of what he wanted more than anything else—to be free of rules, free of this awful desert.

"I don't know *what* to think anymore," Ethan finally said. "When Jeru said we have too many rules, I agreed with him. But then when my father says that rules are important, I believe him, too."

"What about when Leah says rules are important?" Melki asked.

"I want to punch her in the face," Ethan said.

Melki fell face-first into the sand, his body shaking with laughter. Ethan couldn't help laughing, too, even though he hated it when people laughed at their own jokes.

"Come on," Ethan said between chuckles. "Help me get this branch out."

Melki wiped the tears from his eyes, pulled himself up, and grabbed the end of the branch Ethan was holding. "One, two, three—pull," Ethan grunted, yanking back as hard as he could.

The branch slid out of the sand more easily than Ethan had expected. Melki let go in time, but Ethan tumbled backward, pulling the branch, some sand, and a weird-looking black thing about three inches long with him.

The branch flew over his head, the sand rained down on his face and chest, and the black thing landed at his feet. Then it started crawling toward him.

"Look out! It's a scorpion!" Melki yelled.

The large, crab-like insect seemed stunned by its short flight and hard landing. It moved from side to side as it walked and slapped its stinger tail wildly in the sand.

Ethan tried to scream, but it came out sounding like a whimper. He kicked his feet and tried to back away from the deadly insect, but couldn't get a foothold in the ground. All he managed to do was throw a cloud of sand in the air.

The scorpion moved so fast that Ethan didn't have time to kick twice. It scampered across the strap of his sandal and up his leg. Ethan's flesh tingled as he felt the scorpion's hard-shelled body crawling over his ankle and shin. The creature stopped just above Ethan's knee and slowly waved its stinger in the air.

"Don't move!" Melki shouted.

Ethan closed his eyes tightly and tried to control the shiver that was running through his body. He felt the scorpion shift its weight on his leg and knew without looking what was coming. He braced himself for the sting.

*Thwack!*

Ethan opened his eyes and saw Melki standing over him with the tree branch in his hand. Melki pointed to a spot about 20 feet away where the scorpion was lying on its back, writhing and twisting its body as it tried to flip over.

"Thanks," Ethan said weakly, "for not hitting my leg when you swung that thing."

Melki grabbed him by the hand and pulled him up. "Come on," he said, "let's go have some fun."

Still too shaken to move, Ethan watched Melki creep toward the injured scorpion. Melki poked the scorpion with the branch and flipped it over. The insect tried to crawl away, but Melki was too quick for it. With a flick of the branch, he turned it back over. "These things aren't as dangerous as everybody says," Melki explained.

Watching Melki roll the helpless scorpion on the ground, Ethan remembered what his father had told him a few days earlier—that Mount Sinai was like a dangerous scorpion that should be treated with respect. He looked toward Mount Sinai; the dark clouds were still there, along with the thunder and lightning. But the mountain didn't seem quite as scary as it had before. It seemed almost . . . climbable.

"I'm bored," Melki announced, giving the scorpion a final swat. "Let's go explore those hills out beyond the camp over there." He pointed to the area just west of Mount Sinai.

"Okay, but we can't go too far," Ethan said.

"Why, will your father stone us?" Melki asked.

"Stop saying that," Ethan complained. "It's not funny."

"All right, all right," Melki said. "Here, catch." He tossed the tree branch to Ethan. "If you can't make a tent peg out of it, you can save it as a souvenir of your first battle with a scorpion. Now, let's go."

Ethan stared at the ground in front of him as they walked, making sure there were no more scorpions around. Melki stared at the mountain. Neither of them spoke for 15 minutes or so. Finally Ethan broke the silence. "What are you looking for over there?" he asked.

"Some other way up the mountain," Melki answered. "If there's another path somewhere, we won't have to worry about getting past the guards at the boundary marker."

"Do you see anything?" Ethan asked.

"No, it's too steep on this side," Melki answered.

Ethan saw he was right. The west side of Mount Sinai was a sheer wall that rose at least 150 feet straight up before receding into a more rugged, and slightly more horizontal, terrain. "There's no way we could—"

"Shhhh," Melki interrupted, holding up his hand for silence. "Did you hear that?"

Ethan halted, listening. Noises that sounded like a scuffle came from behind a large sand dune to his left.

Then he heard a series of boys' voices:

"You will all bow down before Anubis, the god of the dead!"

"No one is greater than Sobek, the crocodile god!"

"I am Geb, the earth god, and this ground is mine!"

"Ptah is ruler over all!"

These strange announcements were followed by more sounds of fighting, groaning, and grunting.

Ethan looked at Melki and shrugged. Melki put his finger to his lips and motioned for Ethan to follow him. Ethan tried to make his way to the sand dune as quietly as possible, but the strap on his sandal was loose and it slapped against his foot each time he took a step. The scuffling sounds stopped.

Ahead of him, Melki was on his hands and knees, peering as far as he could around the dune. Melki's body froze just for a moment, and Ethan had a sudden urge to run away. But then Melki stood up and brushed the sand off his legs.

Ethan stepped forward and saw four boys about his age, maybe a little older, standing on top of a small hill. They were looking down at him and Melki with their arms folded across their chests.

"We're playing mountain-of-the-gods," one of them explained. "If you want to play, choose a god and try to knock us off the mountain."

"Choose a god?" Ethan asked.

"Yeah," he replied. "I'm Anubis, he's Sobek, he's Geb, and he's Ptah."

Ethan glanced at the players. "Anubis," the one doing the talking, was about Ethan's size and had a front tooth missing. "Sobek" and "Geb" were obviously twins. The only difference between them was that Geb's nose was bleeding. "Ptah" was the biggest of the four by far. He was even bigger than Melki. He had a scratch on his face that ran from the middle of his forehead to the side of his left cheek.

Ethan had never seen any of them before. *Probably from the southern part of camp*, he thought. From the looks of them, he guessed they liked to play rough.

"Okay, I'll be Osiris," Melki announced. Ethan stared at him in shock—not just because he was willing to play, but also because he was able to name an Egyptian god so quickly.

"What about you?" Ptah asked, pointing at Ethan.

Ethan cleared his throat nervously. "Those are all . . . Egyptian gods, aren't they?" he asked.

"Yeah. So what?" Ptah replied. He started down the hill toward Ethan and Melki.

"Um . . . uh . . ." Ethan fumbled. Then he remembered his father's words: *You have a lot of strength,*

*Ethan. . . . It's here and here.* Ethan recalled how his father had touched his head and his chest. He took a deep breath and announced, "Moses said that the God of Israel is the only true God."

Ptah grinned and looked around at his three friends. "Look, it's one of Moses' sheep!"

"I'm not a sheep," Ethan said.

"Baaaaa! I will follow you wherever you go, Moses," the bloody-nosed twin said in a mocking voice. "Baaaaa, I will do whatever you say."

"Baaaaa! Your mother's calling you, little lamb!" his brother added.

"I'm not a lamb!" Ethan yelled.

"Go back to your shepherd, sheep!" Ptah said. Suddenly he charged, his arms straight out and pointed at Ethan's chest.

"Oof!" Ethan grunted as the air was shoved out of his lungs. Losing his balance, he found himself tumbling backwards into the sand.

"Go back to your shepherd if you can *find* your shepherd," Ptah declared. "If he's still alive, he's somewhere up there." He pointed to the top of the mountain.

"Let's show him what we do to Moses' sheep in our part of camp," Anubis suggested with a cackle that made Ethan dread what was coming next.

Ptah reached down and grabbed the front of Ethan's tunic.

"Leave him alone," Melki said. His voice sounded firm, but calm. Ptah let go of Ethan's tunic and turned toward Melki. Ethan scrambled to his feet.

"We've got five players already," Melki said with a friendly smile. "We don't need him. If he doesn't want to play, let him go."

Ptah looked at his three friends and then nodded at Ethan. "Okay, little sheep, we'll let you run along home. But if we see you out wandering around again—"

"We're going to sacrifice you!" Anubis finished. All four of them burst out laughing.

His cheeks burning, Ethan looked to Melki for help. Melki just looked away and started up the hill.

The laughter followed Ethan as he walked away. He clenched his fists and tried to hold back tears. He couldn't decide whether to be grateful to Melki for saving him from a pummeling or to be mad at him for staying behind to play. Ethan's throat seemed to get tighter and tighter as he made his way back to camp.

*That's what I get for trying to obey Moses' rules*, he thought, staring at the sand in front of his feet. *Now all I have is enemies.*

He glanced over his shoulder at the mountain. If he was ever going to be free now, it looked like he'd have to do it himself.

## CHAPTER 6

*I'm trapped*, Ethan thought.

Sitting on a rock in front of his family's tent, he kept thinking about Anubis' warning from the day before: *If we see you out wandering around, we're going to sacrifice you.*

He stopped sharpening the stick he'd found and looked at the flint knife his father had given him. He wished the chipped edge were sharper; this cutting was taking forever . . .

Just then his mother and Leah returned from washing clothes. His mother looked surprised when she saw him. "Ethan, what are you doing home? I thought you would be out playing with Melki."

He sighed, not wanting to admit that Melki had abandoned him yesterday. "Uh . . . I was going to. But I . . . uh . . . thought I would get started on carving the new tent peg that Father wanted."

He could feel Leah giving him a suspicious look, so he kept his gaze on the knife blade.

"Well, I'm glad you're here," his mother said. "You can go to the stream with Leah to get water while I stay here and prepare supper."

Ethan's heart skipped a beat. "I can't leave this area!" he blurted without thinking.

"Why on earth not?" his mom demanded.

"Because . . . Father *really* wants me to finish this tent peg." It was a lame answer, but it was all he could come up with off the top of his head.

"Well, you can finish it when you get back," his mother said as she draped the clothes in her basket over the tent cords to dry.

Leah grabbed the small, clay pitcher and started toward the stream, leaving Ethan the larger—and much heavier—washing bowl to carry. He picked it up and hurried after her, looking around nervously.

"Let's take the shortcut!" he called. If "Ptah" and his friends—whatever their real names were—were out looking for him, they probably would be on the main path that ran through the middle of camp. The shortcut, a trail that wound around people's tents and through their cooking areas, was inconvenient but fairly well hidden.

"Father said we're not allowed to take the short-cut anymore," Leah replied without turning around or slowing down. "He said it bothers too many people."

"Come on, just this once," Ethan pleaded, struggling to get a good grip on the basin and catch up with her at the same time. "Let's stay off the main path."

"No!" Leah said firmly. "You know the rule—no shortcuts. You need to learn to obey."

"And *you* need to learn to be a real person!" Ethan snapped back. "It's no wonder you don't have any friends. You're always trying to be like Father. It's really annoying—and it makes you boring to be around."

Leah stopped dead in her tracks.

*Aw, no*, Ethan thought. *Now she's going to tell Father what I said*. He took a step toward Leah. "Uh, sorry," he mumbled. "I didn't mean—"

"That's Aaron in front of us!" Leah interrupted.

Ethan looked up and saw several dozen people gathered around a tall, bald man who had a bushy, white beard. "Aaron?" Ethan asked. "You mean Moses' brother? What would he be doing in this part of camp?"

"Let's go find out," Leah said as she hurried over toward the group. Ethan paused to look around for potential attackers, then followed.

One of the men in the crowd pointed angrily at Aaron. "This is your responsibility now, Aaron!" he shouted. "Moses is gone, and his God has deserted us.

We need a new god to lead us out of this desert!"

"He's right!" a woman called.

Ethan glanced back and forth as the heads around him nodded in agreement.

"Can you believe they're saying such things to *Aaron?*" Leah whispered. She looked surprised and a little scared.

Ethan shook his head. He *couldn't* believe it. Talking about other gods in front of a powerful leader like Aaron seemed like—well, suicide. If people like Father were ready to stone someone for crossing a boundary line, just think of what they would do to a person who asked for a new god!

Aaron held up his hand for silence. *Uh-oh—here it comes*, Ethan thought.

"I have discussed this matter with several elders in the camp," Aaron said. He seemed tired and a little sad as he fingered the waistcord of his rust-colored robe. "We have decided to honor your request."

All at once the crowd began to cheer and yell. A couple of women hugged each other.

*What's the request?* Ethan wondered. He looked at Leah, who was staring back at him with her mouth wide open.

Aaron held up his hand again and the crowd quieted. "Gather your gold earrings and bring them to the foot of the mountain."

Leah brushed past Ethan and ran back toward the main path. Ethan tried to follow, but the surging crowd got in the way. By the time he reached the path, Leah was out of sight.

Ethan hurried down the path, his grip on the bowl making his fingers ache. All the way to the stream he thought about Aaron's words, but none of them made sense.

When he got to the stream, Leah wasn't there. He looked around to make sure Ptah and his friends weren't nearby, then dipped the bowl in the water and filled it almost to the top.

The journey back to the tent was made in small, painful steps. Filled with water, the bowl was almost too heavy to carry. At one point Ethan wished Ptah and his friends *would* jump out at him—giving him an excuse to drop the bowl and run. But they didn't.

When he finally got back to the tent, Leah and his mother and father were standing out front. Ethan set the water bowl down with a heavy grunt.

"Are you *sure* that's what Aaron said?" his father was asking.

"I'm *positive*, Father," Leah answered. "Ethan was there—he heard it, too."

His father looked at him, and Ethan nodded.

"Mother, will we have to give up our gold earrings?" Leah asked.

"No, you won't," their father answered, anger in his voice. "Because this is a *very* bad idea."

"*What's* a bad idea?" Ethan asked. "What are the earrings *for?*"

"It sounds like Aaron is going to use the gold in the earrings to make some sort of idol," his father explained. "And this family will have no part of any idol. The God of *Israel* is *our* God!"

That night, Ethan lay awake on his mat while the rest of the family slept. He was thinking about earrings and idols, new gods and the God of Israel, Melki and Mount Sinai.

Then he heard the noise.

*Mmmbrmmbmmmbrmm.*

He sat up and looked around. Someone was outside the tent!

The vague mumble of low voices grew clearer. Three, four, five sets of footsteps approached the front of the tent. *It's Ptah and his friends coming to pound me!* he thought, holding his breath. He looked at the goatskin flap that covered the tent entrance and wished it were a lot more solid.

"Amon!" came a shout from outside, and Ethan jumped. "We are here for your gold!"

Ethan could hear his father stirring. "Who disturbs my family at such a late hour?" Father asked.

Three men burst through the tent flap. Leah

screamed. Ethan could see the flame of a small torch carried by one man. The other two grabbed Ethan's father and pulled him to his feet.

Ethan wanted to help his father, but his legs wouldn't move. He could feel himself shaking all over.

"We're here to collect your gold earrings!" one of the men declared. "Aaron needs them."

"What Aaron *needs* is to remember which God led us out of Egypt!" Father growled, pulling himself free of the men's grasp.

"The God of Moses has deserted us," the man said, sounding almost as if he were pleading. "If Aaron doesn't make a new god to lead us, we'll all die in the desert!"

"Enough talk!" the torch-carrier yelled. "Give us your earrings or you *and* your family will be hurt!" He took a step toward Ethan, but Ethan still couldn't move. He watched as the man's face twisted into a frightening sneer.

"Here!" Ethan's mother screamed. She hurled something at the torch-carrier's feet. "Take our earrings and leave us alone!"

With a grunt the torch-carrier bent over and picked up the jewelry. The other two men hurried out of the tent. As he left, the torch-bearer said, "In time you will be glad you helped us."

No one spoke after the men left. Ethan's mother and sister huddled in the corner, sobbing quietly. His father stood in the middle of the tent with his arms at his sides and his fists clenched, muttering to himself.

Still trembling, Ethan rolled over on his side, facing away from his family. He stared at the hairy goatskin of the tent. One question repeated itself over and over in his mind: *Where was the God of Moses just now, when we needed Him?*

*Maybe He* has *deserted us*, Ethan thought.

## CHAPTER 7

For the next week Ethan stuck close to his family's tent. His father helped him carve three new ground pegs from the tree branch Ethan and Melki had found; then father and son dug up the old pegs, anchored the new ones with rocks, and repacked the dirt on top.

His father never mentioned the nighttime intrusion, so Ethan didn't say anything about it, either. What was there to say? Aaron had the earrings and was using them to make an idol. There was nothing anyone could do about it.

*There's nothing I can do about* anything, Ethan thought, slumping in front of the tent with his knife in one hand and a leftover piece of tree branch in the other. *I can't climb the mountain. I can't play with Melki anymore. I can't go exploring, 'cause I might run into Ptah and those guys.*

*I'll never be free*, he thought. *I'm more of a slave than ever.*

All he could do was try to carve this stupid chunk of wood. He held it up and looked at it from different angles, trying to picture a shape he could turn it into. A goose? No, too hard. A fish, maybe?

He sighed. Fish made him think of water. He looked around at the flat, broiling desert and shook his head.

Suddenly his mother emerged from the tent, carrying a pitcher. "I'm going to take some water over to Nathiel. She's been sick for the past couple of days and needs some help. Your father's still at his meeting and your sister's taking a nap. Will you be okay here by yourself?"

"Sure," Ethan said. But he swallowed and looked around for Ptah and his gang.

Noticing that most of the tents seemed deserted, he shifted nervously. "Where *is* everybody, anyway?"

"Probably at the dedication ceremony for the idol," his mother answered. Her large, brown eyes looked sad, but there was an angry edge in her voice.

Ethan sat up, surprised. "The idol is finished already?"

"They've had people working on it night and day," his mother said, staring off toward the mountain. "I heard they melted down the gold, then hammered it into sheets and put those around a piece of wood they'd carved."

Ethan looked down at the chunk of branch in his hand. For a second he wanted to hide it but wasn't sure why.

There was a pause, and finally his mother spoke. "They asked your father to speak at the dedication." Her voice was little more than a whisper. "Your father told Elizah no."

"Elizah the *Judge?*" Ethan asked. "*He's* helping with the idol?"

His mother nodded.

*Then why aren't* we *helping?* Ethan wanted to ask. *If people like Aaron and Elizah think the idol is a good idea, why can't we just accept it? Why does our family always have to be the outcasts? How long are we going to be slaves to God's rules?*

But he knew those questions would hurt his mother. So all he asked was, "Then what are we going to do?"

She looked like she was trying to smile, but it wasn't working. "That's what your father's meeting with four of the elders is about." She hoisted the water pitcher to her shoulder. "I'd better go see Nathiel. Don't cut off your finger with that knife while I'm gone, all right?" she said.

"All right," he repeated. He couldn't think of anything else to say as she turned and started the long trek to the southern part of camp.

As soon as she was gone, Ethan heard a rustling sound behind him. *Ptah!* he thought, and his stomach grabbed. But when he turned, all he saw was Leah poking her head out of the tent.

"I thought you were taking a nap," he mumbled.

"No time to talk," she said loftily, stepping outside and heading for the main path.

"Where are you going?" Ethan called.

"For a walk!" she called back.

Thunder rumbled from the top of the mountain. "No, you're not!" he yelled. "You're going to see the idol!"

She stopped walking.

*Aha!* he thought. *I was right!* Throwing down the knife and wood, he ran after her. "You're going to get in trouble!" he said. "I never thought I'd get to say this to *you*, but you're breaking the rules!"

"No, I'm not!" she cried, putting her hands on her hips. "Father never said I couldn't go."

"Then I'm coming with you," he said. "If it's not wrong for you, it's not wrong for me." *And besides*, he thought, *I don't want to stay here all by myself and get pounded.*

"Do what you please," she said, sounding disgusted. "You always do." She started toward the mountain again, and Ethan followed.

The dedication site was only about 50 paces in

front of the boundary marker. A huge crowd had gathered, but no one seemed to know whether to stand or sit. Ethan squeezed his way to a spot near the front, then groaned when he noticed Leah still at his side.

Aaron, dressed in a fancy yellow robe, stood on a platform that was about five feet high. The only other thing on the platform was a wooden altar about half the size of a family tent, covered by a red cloth. Ethan guessed that the idol was under the cloth.

Aaron, his voice deep but a bit shaky, said a few words about "new beginnings" and "showing us the way out of this wilderness." Ethan only half listened, concentrating instead on looking around for Melki and his mountain-of-the-gods friends.

When Ethan glanced back at the platform, he noticed Aaron was praying. Leah didn't have her head bowed or eyes closed, so Ethan didn't do those things, either.

After the prayer, Aaron walked over to the altar and pulled the cloth away. A cheer went up from the crowd, though Ethan and Leah didn't join in.

The sun, reflecting off the idol's gold surface, shot a blinding glare into Ethan's eyes. He squinted and tried to shield his face, but it didn't work. "What is it, a mountain lion?" he asked Leah.

"A *mountain lion?*" a nearby woman said with

more than a little scorn. "It's a calf!"

"How is a *cow* going to help us get out of the desert?" Leah asked. She didn't seem to be talking to anyone in particular, but spoke loudly enough for everyone around them to hear.

Ethan nudged her with his elbow and gave her a look that he hoped would shut her up.

"It's a *calf*," the woman repeated.

"Oh, *excuse* me," Leah said. "How is a *baby* cow going to get us out of the desert?"

Ethan began to perspire, and it wasn't just the heat. "Come on, Leah," he whispered, pulling at her elbow. "Don't cause a scene."

"I'm not making a scene!" she cried, loudly enough to make Ethan grimace. "I just want to know how a *cow* that's made out of my *earrings* is going to *save* us!"

Two men in front of them turned and stared at Leah. Neither of them looked happy.

Ethan tried to smile at them. "Uh, don't listen to her," he said. "She, uh, hit her head on the way here and she's not thinking clearly."

"Then get her out of here!" one of the men barked.

"Yes, sir!" Ethan said quickly. His hands were trembling as he grabbed her arm. "Come on, Leah, you heard the man. Let's go home and put you to bed. You need your rest."

He pulled her away. She didn't fight as they made their way back through the crowd—but she didn't go quietly, either. "This is *wrong*, and you all know it!" she shouted.

Ethan didn't turn around to see how many people heard her. He didn't really want to know.

When they got to the main path, Leah looked over at him, her nostrils flaring. "Why didn't *you* stand up for what you believe back there?" she asked.

"How do you know *what* I believe?" he shot back.

"Do *you* think those people are doing the right thing?" Her tone made him think that if he said yes, she might pick up a rock and try to stone him on the spot.

He threw up his hands. "I don't know *what* to think!" he cried. "All I know is that we've had a God who gave us rule after rule—and look where it's gotten us." He paused, waiting for the first rock to be thrown. "What if this new god doesn't give us as many rules, and things get better around here?"

Leah looked at him with an expression he couldn't name. It wasn't anger or sadness or disappointment, but a mix of all three.

She didn't say a word the rest of the way home.

And that made Ethan nervous—very nervous.

## CHAPTER 8

*I've gotta get out of here*, Ethan thought later that evening. He was sitting in front of the tent again, carving a small, half-moon wedge from the bottom of his chunk of wood, shaping the area around it into four legs.

The problem was that all the passersby seemed to be staring at his family. Laughing and talking excitedly about tomorrow's Festival of the Golden Calf, the strangers paraded up and down the path—except when they paused to look down their noses at Ethan and his family. One man even stopped for a moment to spit on the ground at the edge of their campsite.

Ethan felt like a leper with oozing sores, rejected by everyone. *Wish I was going with them tomorrow*, he thought. *They have a new god now. They're free to do what they want. The only freedom I have is to be miserable.*

Just then Ethan's father made things worse. Looking up from the sandal he'd been fixing, he announced loudly, "The God of Israel is the *only* God!" Some of the passersby glared at him.

His mother chimed in, setting down the dishes she'd been cleaning. "What will Moses say when he returns?" she asked loudly.

"He will wonder why our people have become so impatient!" his father said in a booming voice. "He will be angry that we allowed our fears to overtake us and that we could not remain faithful until he returned. He will come to us with words from the God of Israel—the only One who can lead us out of this desert!"

Leah, sitting in the doorway of the tent, grinned. She seemed not to care about the disgust and anger on the strangers' faces.

Ethan, however, ducked his head. He wanted to crawl under a rock, bury himself in the sand—anything to escape the stares. *Even running into Ptah and his gang would be better than this*, he thought.

Finally he could stand it no longer. Dropping his knife and wood, he got up. "I, uh, need to stretch my legs a little," he said to no one in particular. "Is it okay if I take a walk?"

His father looked around as if he'd just been awakened from a deep sleep. "A walk? Uh . . . yes, that's fine. Just make sure you head toward the stream and not the mountain."

*I'd head toward the middle of the desert if it were the only way out of here,* Ethan thought. He could feel his family's eyes on him as he walked down the path.

He made his way around a group of women who were twirling and waving scarves. Two small children ran past, singing a song they'd obviously made up themselves about the golden calf.

When he was sure his family could no longer see him, he started running. He thought of the way that man had spat on the ground, and he ran faster. He thought of the men bursting into his family's tent in the middle of the night, and he ran faster still. He thought of all the rules he'd been obeying for so long, and—

And he tripped over the foot someone had stuck in front of him.

As if in a dream, Ethan noticed that his arms and legs were still moving in a running motion as he sailed headfirst across the path. He tried to tuck his shoulder under himself, but it was too late. He landed face first in a pile of sand just off the path.

"Oww," he moaned as his brain scrambled to make sense of what had just happened. He heard cackling laughter behind him, then felt a sinking feeling in the pit of his stomach.

Rolling over, he brushed the sand from his face.

Melki and the four mountain-of-the-gods players were standing over him. None of them seemed worried about whether he was hurt; all had big grins on their faces.

"You should be more careful, running around like that," one of the twins said. He held up his foot. "There are a lot of things you might trip on."

"We saw you coming down the path," his brother explained.

"You were running like one of Moses' little lambs," the biggest one—"Ptah" in the game—said. He grabbed Ethan by the front of his robe and pulled him to his feet. "And we told you what was going to happen if we saw you out wandering around."

"It's time for a *sacrifice!*" the fourth boy yelled. Ethan couldn't remember which god *he* had been.

Melki didn't say anything. But he didn't move to help Ethan, either. He just stood there, watching.

"Let's take him down to the stream and give him a bath!" one of the twins suggested.

"Yeah!" the rest of the boys—even Melki—agreed. Ethan glared at Melki, who seemed not to notice.

"Ptah" and one of the twins gave Ethan a shove in the direction of the stream. Ethan looked for a place to run, but knew he wasn't quick enough to get away from all five of them.

*I'm dead*, he thought.

"You said you were just taking a walk!" The voice came from the path behind them. Ethan turned to see Leah standing there.

*Oh, great*, he thought.

Leah didn't seem to realize what was going on. She pushed her way past Melki and the big guy and stood right in front of Ethan.

"Why are you hanging around with these *rebels?*" Leah asked Ethan in a scornful voice. She looked at Melki. "Your father helped make the idol, didn't he?"

"Yeah, so what?" Melki answered. "It's more than *your* father has done for our people!"

Leah gave Ethan a disapproving look. "What would Father say if he knew you were here with these guys?" she continued. "What do you think *Moses* would say if—"

For a moment Ethan forgot where he was and who was around. He forgot about everything except the look on Leah's face—and he couldn't take it anymore.

"Moses is *dead!*" he yelled.

Leah stepped back and looked at him with wide eyes and a wider mouth. Ethan let fly the words he'd been holding back for weeks, and they felt like little arrows shooting out of his mouth. "He was an old man, and he tried to climb the mountain by himself!

His body is probably splattered all over a bunch of rocks at the bottom of a cliff somewhere. And since Moses is gone, his God is gone, too. But who cares? The only thing Moses' God has done for us since we crossed the Red Sea is lead us deeper into the desert and give us more rules to follow. And I'm sick of following rules! I'm not a slave!"

For a moment he thought she might start crying or slap him. But after looking around the group, she started to say something—and stopped. Then she shook her head and walked away.

*Now I'm really dead,* he thought, his heart beating double-time. *These guys are going to beat me up, and Leah's going to tell Father what I said.*

But when he looked around, he saw that the other boys were all smiling.

"You really told her off!" Melki said with a touch of admiration in his voice.

"That was pretty good, what you said about Moses," one of the twins declared.

"I liked what you said about rules," his brother added.

The big guy stepped forward, and Ethan flinched. But instead of hitting him or grabbing his clothes, the boy put his arm around Ethan's shoulders. "I guess you're not one of Moses' sheep, after all," he said.

Ethan was too stunned to say anything. He'd been

preparing himself for pain, not compliments.

"Hey!" Melki said. "Do you want to head over toward the mountain with us?" The other boys nodded.

"Huh?" Ethan said. *I can't believe they're inviting me to join them—just because I yelled at Leah!*

"We've got a little game we like to play near the idol," one of the twins explained.

For a moment Ethan thought about what his father would say. *What does it matter?* he finally decided. *I'm already in trouble. What's a little more going to hurt?*

"Let's go," he said with a grin.

On the way to the mountain, Ethan found out from Melki that the twins' names were Orek and Patek. The big guy's name was Uli; the other guy's name was Tovar.

"Shhh!" Tovar hissed when they got close to the dedication platform. He pointed to a group of boulders about 20 paces from where the idol stood. Then he got down on his hands and knees and crawled over to them. Ethan and the others followed.

Peering out from behind the rocks, Ethan could see four large torches on the platform, one on each corner. The altar was covered with the red cloth again, and Ethan recognized the outline of the idol underneath.

In the torchlight Ethan saw one man on the platform, another in front of it, and a third to the left of it. He guessed there were also men on the right and behind the platform, but couldn't see them.

The guard on the platform was holding a sword and walking slowly around the altar. The others stared intently into the darkness.

Uli reached into his pocket and pulled out a handful of small rocks. "Everybody take one," he whispered. "The one who comes closest to the guard in front is the winner."

Ethan grabbed his rock quickly so the others wouldn't notice that his hands were shaking. *I wonder how many rules I'm breaking right now?* he thought.

"I'll go first," Orek—or Patek, Ethan couldn't really tell them apart—whispered. He stood up, threw his rock, and fell to his knees in one quick motion.

Ethan listened for it to land, but didn't hear anything. "Too far to the right," Orek or Patek admitted.

"My turn," the other twin said. He stood and threw his rock with the same quick motion his brother had used. Ethan heard it land, but it sounded well short of the target.

"I'll show you how it's done," Melki whispered. He leaned out as far as he could and flung his rock with a quick, sideways motion. Ethan watched as the front guard jumped and started looking around at the ground in front of him.

Ethan snorted and tried to keep from laughing. The rest of the guys were holding their hands over their mouths and shaking silently.

After a minute or so, Uli said, "Now it's *my* turn." He stood up and took aim, not seeming worried about whether anyone saw him. After a quick wind-up, he let the rock go.

Ethan heard the sound of the rock hitting the sand, followed by a loud "Ow!"

"What happened?" the man on the platform yelled.

"Something hit me!" the front guard answered. "I think it was a rock."

"You must have hit him on the bounce," Tovar whispered to Uli.

"Where did it come from?" the platform guard yelled.

Ethan peeked out from behind the rock and saw the front guard looking all around. "I'm not sure!" the guard yelled back.

Uli gave Ethan a lopsided smile. "Your turn," he said.

Ethan nodded and took a step back from the boulder. He brought his hand all the way down to his knee and heaved the stone in a high arc. But as soon as he let it go, he knew he'd thrown it too hard.

*CLANK!*

"You hit the golden calf!" Melki hissed. His eyes were as wide as his smile. The other four guys were grinning, too.

The guard on the platform yelled something Ethan didn't catch. Whatever it was, it scared the other boys enough to send them running in five different directions.

His heart in his throat, Ethan sprang up and ran, too. He could hear the guards yelling behind him. He ran as fast as he could all the way to the main path.

When he got there, he stopped and looked around, panting. A lot of people were standing outside their tents, talking and laughing, but none seemed to be paying attention to him. He let out a deep sigh. After a few moments he headed home with a big smile on his face.

*Now* that's *what freedom is like*, he told himself.

His father, mother, and sister were all in bed when he got back to the tent. In the dark Ethan couldn't tell whether they were asleep. But no one said anything as he made his way to his mat at the back of the tent.

*I guess we'll talk about things in the morning.*

It was not a comforting thought.

## CHAPTER 9

Ethan got up the next morning and helped his family gather manna, just like every other morning. He knelt with his family in the middle of their tent while his father prayed, just like every other morning. He ate a bowl of manna that his mother cooked, just like every other morning.

But to Ethan, it didn't *feel* like every other morning. This morning felt different. *He* felt different—though he couldn't tell exactly what the difference was.

After breakfast, he scooped up his mat and started to head outside to shake the sand from it. His father met him at the tent entrance.

"Put that down and take a seat," his father said. His voice was calm, but the tight lines around his mouth showed anger.

Ethan put the mat down, took a deep breath, and sat cross-legged. *Stay calm*, he told himself. *Just explain that you're tired of being a slave to—*

"What is this?" his father asked, holding out the piece of wood Ethan had been carving.

Ethan swallowed. "Uh . . . It's the piece of wood we used to make—"

"I *know* it's a piece of wood!" his father said. "I'm asking you what you're carving it into!"

Ethan's heart dropped to his stomach. He covered his eyes with his hand so that he wouldn't see his father's reaction. "It's a calf," he said quietly.

"A calf like the one at the foot of the mountain," his father said. Ethan couldn't tell whether it was a question or an observation, so he just nodded.

"Do you know what an idol is, Ethan?" his father asked.

"Yeah, it's a god," Ethan answered.

Reaching down, his father gently lifted Ethan's chin so that they were looking each other straight in the eyes. "No," his father said in a quiet but very firm voice. "An idol is a *pretend* god. It has no power. It's nothing but an ugly statue. The God of—"

"I know what you're going to say," Ethan interrupted. He closed his eyes and took a deep breath, trying to force the next sentence out of his mouth. "The God of rules is the only God."

He opened his eyes and saw that his father's upper lip was beginning to tremble. "*The God of rules?*" his father cried. "This is how you refer to the Lord? Who taught you to be so disrespectful? Your new friends? The ones who laughed when you said those things to your sister last night? Did they teach you to hate the Lord's rules?"

"No!" Ethan protested, his heart hammering. "I've felt this way for a long time! You always talk about the good things the Lord has done, but you never mention how hard He makes our lives with His rules. I feel like I'm still a . . . slave." A bead of sweat rolled down his cheek.

His father stared at him for a moment with sorrow in his eyes. "Rules are like family members, Ethan," he finally said. "You don't know how important they are until they're gone. I don't expect you to understand that now, and I pray that you will never have to find out for yourself."

*If obeying rules is so important*, Ethan thought, *why does it feel so much better to* break *them?* His mind drifted back to last night's adventure. He couldn't help but grin as he recalled the look on Melki's face when that rock hit the golden calf—

"Is this *funny* to you?" His father's angry voice brought Ethan back to reality. "This camp is being torn apart by people who don't want to obey God's rules. I will not let *you* become one of them!" His father gave him one more stern look and walked out of the tent.

Exhaling loudly, Ethan flopped back on his mat and looked up at the patched tent ceiling. *If Father only knew how fun it is to be free of rules, he'd probably change his mind.* He lay there for what seemed like a long time, remembering the night before and snickering softly.

Finally he left the tent and looked around for his family. *Probably went to wash their clothes,* he thought. *I guess they don't want me around right now.*

Thunder from the top of Mount Sinai echoed through the camp. *If I head toward the mountain,* Ethan thought, *I might find Melki and the rest of the guys. We could laugh about last night—and plan more fun stuff.*

He scanned the empty campsite. "Well, my family deserted me," he said out loud. "I think I'll desert *them* for a while." He started walking toward the mountain.

On the way he passed several people who looked like they were dressed for the evening festival. Some had already begun celebrating. They were laughing and dancing in front of their tents. A few were drinking from long, leather wine pouches. Ethan smiled and waved as he passed by. *That's how free people live,* he thought. *Look how much fun they're having.*

The scene at the foot of the mountain had

changed since last night. In place of the guards, dozens of men waited near the platform. Some held birds, others held lambs, and at least two held goats. None of the animals were moving. *They're offering burnt sacrifices*, Ethan thought, *just like we used to do for Moses' God.*

The golden calf now rested on a stand at the back of the platform. The altar, with a fire burning on top of it, sat just in front of the idol. Aaron stood before the altar, dressed in the same fancy yellow robe he'd worn at the dedication ceremony.

At the edge of the crowd, not far from last night's hiding place, Ethan found a small rock. He sat, glad he could see everything that was going on.

*You shouldn't be here*, a little voice in his head told him.

Ethan ignored it.

One at a time each man in line carried his dead animal to the platform and handed it to Aaron. Aaron cut each animal's body into four pieces and threw them into the fire. Aaron worked quickly, Ethan noticed—much less carefully than the priests who offered sacrifices to Moses' God.

Ethan thought about the first time his father had let him watch a burnt offering ceremony. He remembered the thrill of sneaking away to one of the slave quarters in Egypt, where a secret altar had been set up. He also remembered the warm, peaceful feeling he had as he watched the priest pray over the offering and ask the Lord to receive it. "This sacrifice is the way we receive forgiveness for our sins," his father had explained.

A pang of guilt stabbed at Ethan's stomach. *There probably aren't enough animals in the whole camp to make up for all the rules I've broken.* But then he reminded himself: *If I'm free from rules, I don't have to worry about breaking them.*

Looking up, he noticed that the next man on the platform with Aaron wasn't holding an animal. He was holding a wineskin. Aaron shook his head and held out his hands to stop the man. But the man just pushed him away and danced around the platform for a minute or so with the wineskin over his head, while Aaron shook his head and watched. Then the man walked over to the altar and poured his wine in the fire.

*Whoosh!* The flames shot at least 10 feet in the air. The crowd oohed and aahed; some people clapped. The man then jumped off the platform and started dancing in front of it.

Another man climbed onto the platform and took off his robe. Dressed only in a loincloth, he started tearing the robe apart and throwing the pieces in the fire. Meanwhile, the men who were waiting to offer *real* sacrifices seemed to be getting impatient. Two of them tried to get on the platform at the same time, then started yelling and shoving each other. Finally one man pushed the other off the platform to the ground below, and the crowd clapped and cheered.

Ethan's stomach churned. *Why are they acting this way?* he wondered. *This is supposed to be a serious ceremony.*

Suddenly he felt someone grab the back of his shirt. Looking up, he saw a man holding a wineskin over his head. "Our new god has commanded you to drink!" the man said, slurring his words. Before Ethan could move, purple wetness came raining down, splashing his forehead, soaking his hair.

Gasping, he yanked himself free and stood up. Wine dripped from his hair into his face. The smell reminded him of rotting manna, and the churning in his stomach grew worse.

The man looked at Ethan and started laughing. Losing his balance, the man fell hard on his rear end—but the laughter didn't stop.

Trembling, Ethan backed away. All around him he saw dozens, maybe hundreds of people joining the celebration. "Hail to our new god!" someone yelled. A man was on his knees, arms stretched over his head, eyes closed, swaying from side to side. A woman wearing a pink veil over her face was dancing around him.

Ethan took a couple of steps to his left and bumped into a large, beefy man who had a neatly trimmed black beard. "Why aren't you worshiping, boy?" the man growled.

Ethan tried to say something, but couldn't. All he could think about were the purple stripes painted on the man's face and neck.

"I . . . I . . . just want to go home," Ethan stammered.

He turned and ran as fast as he could back toward the main path. He glanced behind him a couple of times to make sure no one was following him, but all the people he saw were heading *toward* the mountain, not away from it. Gulping air, he ran all the way home.

When he got there, panting and wincing at the pain in his side, his family's campsite still seemed deserted. *Where could they be?* he wondered, bending over to catch his breath.

Just then he heard noises coming from inside the tent. Was it somebody moaning? Crying? Afraid of what he might find, he walked slowly to the open flap and looked in.

He gasped. His father was lying on his back in the middle of the tent, a large bump in the middle of his forehead and a dark bruise near his temple. His eyes were swollen shut, his upper lip split almost to his nose. Blood was matted in his hair, dried on his cheek, dripping from his ear.

His mother was kneeling over his father, gently wiping his face with a wet cloth. Her head and shoulders were shaking, and Ethan could hear her quiet sobs.

"W-what happened?" Ethan asked. His eyes began to water so much that his father's face looked blurry.

His mother turned toward him. "Three men attacked him on the way to the stream," she said, wiping the tears from her cheeks. "They beat him with clubs and kicked him."

Ethan felt his jaw clench. "*Why?*"

"They said he was a traitor. They said if he didn't change his mind about Aaron's idol, the whole camp was in danger. They warned him to stop worrying about commands that didn't matter anymore."

Ethan looked down at the ground. He could feel the tears in his eyes start to spill over.

Blinking, he brushed his cheeks with the back of his hand and looked around the tent. "Where's Leah?" he asked hoarsely.

"She went to find you," his mother answered. "She said she knew where you would be."

He froze. Leah was walking by herself through that mob in front of the mountain? The thought made him sick to his stomach.

*And it's my fault that she's there, looking for me,* he thought.

"I've got to go find her," he said as he ran out of the tent.

## CHAPTER 10

*Rules are like family members, Ethan. You don't know how important they are until they're gone.*

His father's words had sounded so ridiculous this morning. So why were they rattling around in his head now, while he was half-walking, half-running to find his sister?

*Leah's not gone,* he told himself. *She's at the mountain, probably making fun of someone for worshiping a cow.* He pictured her, with her fake grown-up voice and know-it-all expression, arguing with someone three times her age about obeying the Lord's rules. And for the first time he could remember, that image didn't make him want to punch her.

*Please, God, help her to be okay.*

"Moses and his God are dead!"

Ethan stopped to see where the shouting was coming from. Two men ran from a tent just ahead of him. "Long live the new god of Israel!" one of them yelled. He kicked over a large boiling pot in front of the tent and sent water running everywhere.

"What are you looking at?" the second man shouted. He was holding a club and staring at Ethan.

Ethan felt his palms get sweaty. "I was just—"

He stopped. There was blood dripping from the end of the stick.

Shuddering, he started down the path again. *I've seen enough blood for one day*, he thought.

A long rumble of thunder rolled from the top of Mount Sinai. All at once Ethan pictured someone at the festival pulling out a club and beating Leah bloody for speaking out against the golden calf.

His heart skipped a beat. *It's your fault she's there*, he told himself. *She's looking for you.*

He started running—and felt the pain immediately. The muscles in his legs cramped and his lungs felt as if they were on fire. *Wish I hadn't run all the way home*, he thought. But he didn't slow down. He couldn't.

Out of the corner of his eye he spotted something moving on the mountain, about halfway between the bottom of the clouds and the ground. Whatever it was disappeared behind a ridge. A mountain lion, he guessed. *Better not let Father see it—he might try to stone it to death for being on the mountain.*

For a second he smiled. But then he remembered

the blood dripping from his father's ear, and he ran faster.

*If I were Leah, where would I look for me?* he wondered. He flinched at the thought of actually *being* Leah—doing nothing but cleaning clothes, washing dishes, and fetching water all day. *No wonder she thinks about rules all the time. Maybe they're the only thing that makes her life interesting.*

His legs were aching so much he had to slow down. Soon he had to walk anyway, as the path was clogged with people. In the distance he could hear trumpet blasts and screaming festival-goers. The sounds reminded him of celebrations in Egypt—the ones his father always pulled him away from. "People who worship strange gods do strange things," his father would say. "Things you should never see."

Ethan gazed around, shaking his head. Those Egyptian festivals couldn't have been any stranger than what he was seeing now. To his right, two men were dancing together. To his left, a group of women were throwing themselves, face first, onto the sandy ground.

In the distance, shadows of the mountain were creeping across the Sinai Valley. The platform was already in the shade. *It's getting late,* he realized. *It's going to be dark soon.* His heart raced. *There's no way I'll be able to find her in the dark!*

Desperate for just a glimpse of her, Ethan clambered to the top of one of the boulders that he and the other boys had hidden behind. Moments later he looked out over the entire crowd. But where was Leah?

He glanced at the sky. The sun was getting lower and lower. "What am I going to do?" he murmured. "I'm running out of time. There's no way—"

"Eeeethaaan! Eeeethaaan!"

His eyes widened. Leah's voice!

"Eeeethaaan! Eeeethaaan!" Her voice didn't sound as loud this time. She was getting further away!

He scanned the crowd as quickly as he could, looking for anyone who seemed to be out of place. He started on the right side of the mob, slowly working his eyes across the middle. When he got all the way to the left side, he started back on the right. Once, twice, three times he repeated the process—but without success.

His heart was in his throat as he turned his head to the right for a fourth time. Just then he caught a glimpse of a girl about Leah's height; she walked slowly on the left fringe of the crowd. Her head kept moving from side to side, as though she were looking for someone. Ethan saw her cup both hands around her mouth.

"Eeeethaaan! Eeeethaaan!"

"Leah!" he yelled. He jumped up and waved his arms even though she was walking away from him. She didn't turn around. He looked again to make sure it really was her.

"Le—" This time the word stuck in his throat.

From his perch on the rock, Ethan watched as five boys sneaked up behind Leah. He didn't need to see their faces to know who they were.

"Leah, look out!" he yelled. He stepped to the edge of the boulder. It was a long way down, but he'd have to jump anyway. Holding his breath, he leaped—and felt the back of his robe brush the rock as he fell, and fell, and fell.

"Ooomph!" He landed on his feet, crouching. *Ow!* he thought. The sandy ground was harder than it looked. His knees and ankles tingled as he tried to stand up.

"Nice jump, boy!" a man in the crowd yelled.

"Do it again!" a woman added.

A huge crash of thunder shook the valley. Ethan noticed that the clouds on top of the mountain were much darker than he'd ever seen them. They rolled over and around each other as though stirred by a giant, invisible hand. Even though the sun had not set, it looked like late evening in the valley, and the glow of burning torches on the platform caught Ethan's eye.

Jolts of pain shot through his ankles as he started to run in Leah's direction. He tried to shift his weight back and forth as he ran, and that seemed to ease the pain a little.

*I must look pretty strange to these people*, he thought, as he half-galloped, half-waddled his way through the crowd. A woman who looked to be about his mother's age fell to her knees in front of him and began waving her arms in the air. "Save us, save us," she chanted.

*Okay, maybe I* don't *look strange to these people*, he thought, making a wide circle around her.

When he finally reached the edge of the crowd, he heard Leah's voice above the singing and shouting.

"Let go of me, Melki! What are you guys doing?"

Ethan breathed a short sigh of relief. She sounded more annoyed than worried.

He pushed his way through the last few people in the crowd, out into the open, and looked around. Uli, Melki, Orek, Patek, Tovar, and Leah were standing less than 10 paces away on his right. Uli and Melki were holding Leah's arms.

Melki smiled and motioned for Ethan to come closer. "Look what we found out wandering around," he said.

"I can't believe you're in on this!" Leah said when she saw Ethan. "I thought you'd stopped wasting your time with these rebels."

*I came to rescue you!* he wanted to yell. *I nearly broke both of my ankles jumping off a boulder to get here in time!* But he didn't say anything. He just stared at her, trying to think of a plan to get them both home safely.

Finally, he asked, "What are you guys doing?" His hands and legs were shaking, but he tried to keep his voice calm.

"We're going to play mountain-of-the-gods again," Uli answered. He had a smile on his face, but his voice sounded mean. "Only this time we're going to use a *real* mountain."

"Melki told us about your plan to climb the mountain and get a closer look at the lightning," Tovar explained. "It sounded like a good idea."

"We heard the boundary guards are gone," Melki said. "Now that Moses is out of the picture, nobody cares who crosses it anymore." He glanced at the struggling Leah and snickered. "Well, almost nobody."

"A rule is a rule!" Leah said through gritted teeth. "God will punish anyone who crosses that boundary. Maybe He'll even strike them with lightning."

Melki laughed. "Yeah, right. You'd like that, wouldn't you, Leah the Law Lover?"

Uli grinned. "Well, there's only one way to find

out. Let's test your theory, Law Lover."

Ethan's mouth went dry. "What do you mean, *test* it?" he asked.

"Let's take your sister over the boundary and see what happens," Uli replied.

"No!" Leah yelled. She tried to jerk her arms free, but Uli and Melki held tight. She looked at Ethan. "This isn't funny," she said. "You shouldn't even joke about things like that."

"Who's joking?" said one of the twins.

"Come on, Ethan," Melki said, "she's been making our lives miserable since we left Egypt. Let's show her what happens when she breaks one of Moses' precious rules."

"Yeah," said the other twin. "*Nothing* happens."

Melki and Uli started dragging Leah up the path toward the boundary marker. Her eyes got wide and her mouth dropped open. She twisted her body and tried to fall to the ground, but Melki and Uli wouldn't let go.

"Noooooooo!" she cried.

*You've got to* do *something!* Ethan told himself. *Now!*

"Let her go!" he screamed.

Melki and Uli stopped and stared at Ethan. Tovar and the twins stared, too.

"Ethan!" Melki said, sounding exasperated. "I

thought you were with *us!*"

Ethan swallowed. "So did I."

"You're sick of rules, remember?" Melki said. "You said so yourself about a million times."

Ethan lowered his gaze to the path. "That was before I saw what happens when the rules are gone," he said, so softly he could barely hear himself. In his mind he saw his father lying in the tent, bleeding.

He looked up to see Uli's angry face. "Hold her," Uli told Tovar. "Make sure she doesn't get away."

Tovar grabbed Leah's arm. She didn't try to escape. She didn't even look at Ethan.

*She's probably praying,* Ethan thought. He glanced up at the storm clouds on the mountain and thought again about the invisible hand that seemed to be stirring them. *Lord, if You are still up there, please—*

Before he could finish, Uli grabbed him by the front of his robe and swung him toward the ground. Ethan tried to catch himself, but couldn't. He landed on his back with a spine-rattling jolt. Uli planted his fists firmly on Ethan's chest.

"I *knew* you were one of Moses' sheep," Uli growled.

"It's . . . better than being . . . one of Aaron's donkeys," Ethan managed. With Uli pressing down on his chest, the words came out muffled and breathless. But

Uli heard them, and tiny splotches of red appeared on his cheeks and forehead, spreading until his entire face looked sunburned.

"Get up," Uli snarled, grabbing a handful of Ethan's hair and giving it a yank.

"Oww!" Ethan yelled. He grabbed Uli's left arm, the one that was clutching his hair, and managed to pull himself up to a standing position. His eyes watered and his scalp tingled.

He looked over at the adults who were dancing and chanting less than 20 feet away. A couple of them watched his struggle with smiles on their faces. *Why don't they do something?* Ethan wondered.

"Help!" he yelled. "They're going to—"

Uli grabbed Ethan's right arm and twisted it behind his back so that Ethan's knuckles were almost touching his shoulder.

His shoulder felt as if it had burst into flame. He tried to groan, but no sound came out. The burning sensation shot down his arm to his elbow, then back up to his wrist. He still couldn't make a sound, but he couldn't stop the tears from rolling down his cheeks, either.

"Let's take *both* of them to the mountain!" one of the twins yelled.

Ethan looked up and saw a jagged bolt of light-

ning explode through the clouds and disappear behind the mountain.

"Maybe the next one is coming for *you*," Uli
whispered in his ear.

Thunder rolled like boulders from the mountain, the deep sounds seeming to find their target in Ethan's chest. As Uli pushed him up the path, he could see bright bolts of lightning striking faster and more furiously than ever.

He could barely breathe, but now it wasn't from excitement. *A few days ago, this was the only place in the world I wanted to be,* he thought. *Now it's the last place in the world I want to be.*

He tried to laugh, but it came out as a sob.

"I think he's crying!" Uli announced.

Ethan could hear Tovar and the twins laughing behind him. He wondered what Melki and Leah were thinking.

*Leah,* Ethan thought. *If it weren't for her, I might have a chance. I could try to fight my way out or at least try to run away and get lost in the crowd. But as long as they have her—*

He had to think of something, and fast.

Something that would get the other boys to let Leah go.

His heart pounded as they neared the boundary marker. *No guards*, he thought, looking around. The men had been a pain when he'd wanted to go up the mountain, but now he wished they were still here.

The flashes of lightning were coming even faster, flooding the landscape in blue-white brightness. *Maybe we won't get hit*, he told himself. *Moses never said we'd be struck by lightning if we crossed the line.* But he felt another tear trickle down his cheek anyway.

*Wish I were braver*, he thought. Suddenly that gave him an idea.

"Hey, Tovar," he called out. "Has Uli always been a coward?"

"Coward?" Uli yelled. He pushed up on Ethan's arm, still bent behind his back. A hot pain shot through the entire right side of Ethan's body.

"Yeah . . . a . . . coward," Ethan groaned. "You're afraid to go up the mountain yourself, so you're making a girl do it for you."

Uli let go of Ethan's arm and spun him around so that they were face to face. Ethan breathed a silent sigh of relief and wiggled his arm, trying to get the blood flowing again.

"I'll show *you* who's a coward," Uli said. He gave

Ethan a shove, then stepped toward him. Ethan looked back and saw that the boundary marker was only about 15 feet away.

"Let her go!" Uli yelled back over his shoulder. "Otherwise he might start *crying* again. *I'll* go up the mountain with him. I'm not afraid of Moses' God."

Melki and Tovar glanced at each other, shrugged, and let go of Leah's arms. She just stood there, staring at Ethan, looking scared and confused.

"Run, Leah!" Ethan yelled. "Run home! Don't stop until you get there!" The tone of his voice seemed to snap Leah out of her trance. She looked at Ethan one last time, then pushed Tovar out of her way and ran back toward the festival crowd.

"Ow!" cried Ethan as Uli shoved him in the chest again. Ethan stumbled backwards, but kept his balance.

The boundary marker was now almost close enough to touch. Ethan noticed that Melki, Tovar, and the twins stayed where they were.

"Listen, Uli," Ethan said, gazing worriedly at the stack of stones. "Something bad's going to happen if we cross that boundary. We might not get struck by lightning—but if someone sees us, they might take us out and stone us."

Uli snorted. "Who's the donkey *now?*" He pointed to the festival crowd. "Do you think anyone down there is going to care if we cross this stupid line? Look at them! We have a new god. We don't have to worry about Moses' rules anymore."

More thunder rumbled overhead. "I *am* looking at them," Ethan said, starting to feel dizzy. "The whole camp is a mess. Maybe God gives rules for a reason. Maybe He doesn't want us on the mountain because He's holy, and—"

Before he could say anything else, Uli turned and gave him one more shove. Instead of stumbling backwards this time, Ethan fell to the ground. He stuck his rear end out to absorb most of the impact, and managed to get his elbows behind him in time to keep from hitting his head on the ground.

In an instant Uli was on top of him, straddling his stomach. Ethan squinted at the boundary marker and saw that his shoulders were even with the back of the stone pile. His heart jumped. *If my head touches the ground—*

Uli looked over at the boundary marker and smiled. He put his left arm on Ethan's chest and his right hand on Ethan's forehead. "Here we go, Sheep Boy!" he said.

"Don't . . . do it!" Ethan grunted. He could feel the veins in his neck standing out as he strained to keep his head off the ground. "Whatever happens to me is going to happen to—"

*CR-RRR-AAAAAAA-CK!*

Ethan felt the explosion in the pit of his stomach before the sound of it reached his ears. The noise was so sharp, so clear, and so loud that it made the hair on his arms and neck stand on end.

The ground below his shoulders rattled. Small chunks of rock, dirt, and sand pelted the side of his face.

Screaming, Uli tried to cover his head with his arms. Ethan couldn't tell if the boy had been hit or not.

Using every bit of strength he had left, Ethan lifted his hips and flipped himself over. Uli lost his balance and fell onto his left shoulder. Ethan expected him to get up and charge again, but Uli just lay there with arms still covering his head and his knees drawn up to his chest.

*Get away from the mountain!* a voice in Ethan's head shouted. He tried to lift himself, but his arms felt like loose tent straps. He collapsed face-first back into the sand.

A deep roll of thunder started overhead. *Oh no,* he thought, *here comes more lightning!* He squeezed his eyes tight, covered his head with his hands, and braced himself.

But nothing happened.

Ethan lifted his face from the sand and listened.

Everything was quiet. The singing and dancing had stopped.

He looked back at Melki, Tovar, and the twins. None were moving. They stared in Ethan's direction with their mouths open.

*What's wrong?* he wondered. *Am I on fire?* He reached back and patted the back of his robe, but didn't feel any flames.

All at once he realized they weren't staring at him. They were staring at something *behind* him. He turned slowly to look, not sure he wanted to see what was there.

*"Moses!"*

Only after the word was out of his mouth did Ethan realize he had said it.

The old man looked down at Ethan, then back at the crowd. He was standing about 15 feet past the boundary marker. The long, silver beard looked longer than ever; the white cloak with the up-and-down purple stripes was dusty and wrinkled. He was still as a statue—except for his nostrils, which flared like an angry bull's, and his eyes, which seemed to move from person to person in the crowd.

Ethan lowered his head and noticed something on the ground at Moses' feet. At first it just looked like rocks, but then he realized they were pieces of a whole. The whole was a flat rock carved with some kind of writing. It reminded him of stone tablets he'd seen in Egypt, the ones chiseled with symbols like eyes and birds and names of pharoahs.

*Are those God's rules?* he wondered.

All at once he realized what had happened. *That must have been the crash we heard. It wasn't lightning striking—it was stone breaking. Moses must have dropped the tablets—or thrown them down—when he saw the idol!*

Out of the corner of his eye, Ethan saw a wobbly Uli stand up, look around, and sneak off—away from Moses and the crowd. Melki and the other boys just watched him go.

A moment later Ethan realized he was still lying on the ground. Standing stiffly, he brushed the sand from the front of his robe. He heard someone in the crowd murmur and saw that Moses was coming toward the boundary marker.

Backing away from the pile of rocks, Ethan gave Moses room to pass. *He moves fast for an old man*, Ethan thought numbly. *Especially one who's spent the last 40 days mountain climbing.*

The old man didn't seem to notice him. Ethan fell in step behind Moses, figuring that if Melki or the others had anything planned, the safest place to be was in the Israelite leader's shadow.

But as Ethan passed the other boys, the way they

all looked down at their sandals made him think he wouldn't have to worry about them any longer.

The crowd at the foot of the mountain backed away as Moses got closer. Ethan couldn't tell whether they were angry because their festival was over or whether they were afraid of what was going to happen to them.

As the crowd fell back, Ethan saw Leah waiting for him with a grin on her face.

"I thought I told you to run home," he said.

"I didn't know that was a rule," Leah replied. "Otherwise, I would have obeyed you." Her smile faded. "The reason I came looking for you was to tell you that something's happened to Father. He—"

*Father—I almost forgot!* "I know what happened," Ethan said. "We've got to get back there—now!"

## CHAPTER 12

It was nearly dark by the time Ethan and Leah got back to the tent. Ethan paused at the tent entrance and took a deep breath.

*What if he's dead?* he thought. He looked over at Leah. She shook her head as though she knew what he was thinking.

The air inside the tent was sour, like the smell of traveling clothes that hadn't been washed for a week. His father lay on his mat just across from the entrance. His mother lay on the ground next to him. Judging by the drag marks on the floor, Ethan guessed that his mother had moved his father by herself.

"I'm . . . so glad you two are home," his mother mumbled. She sounded more asleep than awake. "We've been worried sick about you."

"How's Father?" Leah whispered.

"The bleeding's stopped," his mother said wearily. "He needs rest. We all do. We'll talk about it in the morning."

Ethan limped over to his mat and plopped down on his back. His ankles were throbbing, his shoulder was stiff, and the skin on the back of his head was still tingling. He couldn't help letting out a groan.

"Are you okay?" Leah whispered, kneeling at the foot of his mat.

"Yeah, I think so," Ethan said.

"I . . . uh . . . just wanted to say thanks for coming to help me," Leah said. She kept her eyes on the ground in front of her while she talked.

"It's okay," he whispered, wincing at a pain in his arm. "After all, family members are like rules—you don't know how important they are until they're gone."

"Huh?" she said.

"Never mind. We'd better stop talking so Father can sleep. I'll see you in the morning."

"Right."

Ethan closed his eyes. In the distance, he heard a sharp crack of thunder. *It's not over yet*, he thought, and a shiver ran down his spine.

The next morning Ethan woke to the sound of voices outside the tent. He glanced around and saw that everyone else was up already. Bright sunlight flooded the tent through the open flaps.

*Father!* he remembered. He tried to get up quickly, but his ankles and shoulder wouldn't let him.

After a couple of tries he managed to pull himself up using one of the tent posts for support. He hobbled over to the entrance, trying to adjust his eyes to the brightness.

Outside, his father was sitting on a rock. He still had some scabs and bruises on his face, but most of the swelling was gone. Leah was wiping his face with a wet cloth. Ethan's mother was standing over the cooking pot, stirring. The smell of fresh manna made Ethan's stomach rumble.

*I guess manna's not so bad*, he thought. *Better than sand, anyway.*

His father noticed him in the doorway and tried to smile, but the muscles in his face seemed frozen. "Leah told me what happened," he said. "I'm proud of you, son." Only one side of his mouth moved when he talked.

Ethan's eyes filled with tears. "It's not right," he said. "It's not right what they did to you."

His father looked into the distance and shook his head. "I would not want to be in their place," he said. "They will pay a high price for disobeying the God of Israel."

There was a long pause, and Leah finally spoke. "Some of the elders came by this morning to see Father," she told Ethan. "They said that after we left, Moses threw the golden calf in the fire. He told Aaron and his followers that they're going to be punished for what they did."

Ethan stared at Leah. For once she didn't sound glad that the rule-breakers would be punished. In fact, she sounded sad.

"I know Melki was your friend, Ethan," she said. "I'm sorry."

Ethan looked at the flames of the cooking fire. He thought about Uli and Tovar, Orek and Patek, Elizah the Judge and the man with the stripes painted on his face. But mostly he thought about Melki and his family.

*I came close to being one of them*, he thought.

None of them said anything for a long time. At last Ethan cleared his throat. "Will it always be like this?" he asked. "Will we always wander in the desert? Won't we ever have a real home?"

His father turned toward him, and his eyes shone. "Someday," he said. "Someday, Ethan. A land flowing with milk and honey. That's the Lord's promise."

Ethan lifted his eyes toward Mount Sinai. *Maybe if God can bring Moses back after that long on the mountain, He can take us to the promised land, too. Maybe.*

"And the new rules?" he asked. "What will they be like?"

"I don't know," his father said. "But I do know they'll be for our good."

Ethan nodded slightly, remembering the chaos in the camp. *I wanted to be free, like those people*, he thought. *But they weren't free at all.*

He sighed. This was going to take time, learning how to be free. But he had the feeling the answer had something to do with following the God of Israel—not running away from Him.

"Speaking of rules," his mother said, handing Ethan a bowl of cooked manna, "this morning the men said Moses is going back up the mountain. He broke the tablets that the rules were written on, so the Lord is going to give him new ones."

Ethan remembered the shattered tablets he'd seen. *So those* were *the new rules.*

Leah spoke up. "And I promise not to nag you about them," she said. "After last night, I can see you don't need my help to obey."

"Of *course* I don't," Ethan said, grinning. "As long as there aren't too *many* new rules."

His father chuckled. "And how many is *too* many?" he asked.

Ethan thought for a moment. "Oh . . . as long as it's less than *10* I should be okay," he said.

"Hmm," his mother said with a smile. "We'll see, Ethan. We'll see."

## Letters From Our Readers

Which parts of this story really happened?

Pam C., Nashville, TN

You'll find the true story of this time in the Book of Exodus, chapters 19, 20, and 32. The Israelites, having been freed from slavery in Egypt, had been in the wilderness for about three months when Moses went up the mountain to receive new laws from God. People aren't sure now which mountain was Mount Sinai, though tradition favors a peak called Jebel Musa in the southern Sinai Desert. The people prepared by washing their clothes, as in this story; they saw the lightning and clouds and smoke, and heard the thunder and trumpet blast and God's voice. Because God had come to the mountain, it was holy—which was why everyone except Moses was banned from climbing it. The penalty was being stoned or shot with arrows. As in the story, most of the Israelites rebelled while Moses was gone; they worshiped the golden calf Aaron had made. Moses reacted by smashing the stone tablets. Except for Moses and Aaron, the characters in the story are fictional. Ethan's family represents those who stayed loyal to God; Melki and the other boys reflect the attitude of those who turned away from the Lord.

What was manna, anyway?

Brady S., Red Deer, Alberta, Canada

So that the Israelites wouldn't starve in the desert, God provided food. This food was manna, a white, flaky substance that appeared on the ground in the morning and melted away in the heat of the day. The people collected manna, ground it up, and boiled it or baked it into cakes. The flavor was like wafers made with honey (Exodus 16:31) and like something made with olive oil (Numbers 11:8). There were rules about gathering manna. Each morning, people were to pick up only what they needed for the day—about three quarts per person. If they gathered too much and saved it for the next day, it would go bad—getting smelly and full of worms. The only exception was the sixth day of the week, when people were to gather twice as much as usual and save half—so that they wouldn't have to collect it on the Sabbath, a day of rest. God did provide quail to eat when the Israelites complained about their manna diet (Exodus 16:13), but they ate manna for 40 years!

What rules were on the stone tablets?

Chris D. and Jon D., Flushing, NY

God gave Moses many commands (see Exodus 21–31), but it's generally thought that those on the tablets were the Ten Commandments (Exodus 20). The custom at the time was to make two copies of legal agreements, so each tablet would have contained all of the Ten, written on the front and back by God Himself (Exodus 32:15–16). Writing on stone tablets wasn't unusual in those days; the ancient Code of Hammurabi, a Babylonian ruler, included a seven-foot slab recording more than 280 laws!

What happened to families like Melki's who rebelled against God?

Wesley W., Wheaton, IL

After Moses smashed the stone tablets, he burned the golden calf, ground it to powder, sprinkled the powder on the water, and made the people drink it (Exodus 32:19–20). When some of the Israelites remained out of control, Moses stood at the camp entrance and called, "Whoever is for the LORD, come to me" (Exodus 32:26). Men from the Levite tribe responded; Moses told them to take up swords and kill those who were still rebelling. About 3,000 people died that day. Later the Lord struck the people with a plague—a disease—as punishment for worshiping the idol (Exodus 32:35). What happened to families like Melki's may depend on whether they continued to disobey God. The punishments may seem harsh, but the sin was very serious. Worshiping the idol was rejecting God; if He had not dealt firmly with the rebellion, it probably would have spread, ruining the whole nation's chances of ever being His people and living in the land He had promised them.

Did families like Ethan's ever get out of the desert?

Kurt B., Colorado Springs, CO

Yes and no. The Israelites continued to wander in the desert for 40 years, often grumbling and disobeying. God may have let them do this because they weren't ready to enter the homeland He'd promised. Most of the people who'd left Egypt as grown-ups must have died before the desert days were over; kids like Ethan could have survived to see the "land flowing with milk and honey" (Exodus 3:8). God used these hard years to teach the Israelites many things, just as He sometimes uses our hard times to help us learn to depend on and obey Him.